必考片語問題集

劉慧如
Tom Brink 編著

ESSENTIAL TOEIC PHRASE

隨身攜帶！隨時學習！

書泉出版社 印行

Preface / 作者序

「1日1分鐘」新多益叢書在第一本單字書出版後，非常感謝讀者們的支持與鼓勵，雖然當中仍有些許瑕疵，但承蒙大家的海涵，仍然給予我們繼續進步的空間與機會，在聽取了大家的建議與意見後，我們第二本推出的是片語書，有鑑於同學們在應考多益時，問題大多來自於字彙、片語及文法，我們特別以此作為我們叢書推出的順序，希望能夠對考生帶來有效率的協助。

在這裡除了再次感謝五南出版社的編輯大人之外，也要感謝這本書的合作作者Tom Brink，Tom是位非常有經驗的作者及編輯，慧

如非常珍惜這次與他的合作，他雖是位在台灣的外籍老師，但他的中文造詣卻也十分令人驚豔，也讓慧如學到了許多，再次感謝他，本書從撰寫到錄製都是我們兩人攜手完成，希望大家能從中有所收穫！

最後，在這裡提醒大家，隨手帶著這本口袋書，多念多記、多練習，「Practice makes perfect！」是任何學習的亙古不變的真理，只要努力，相信您的多益分數，絕對能步步高升，只要認真，也一定可以出師就告捷哦！讓我們為大家加油囉！

慧如於華岡　2012/1/6

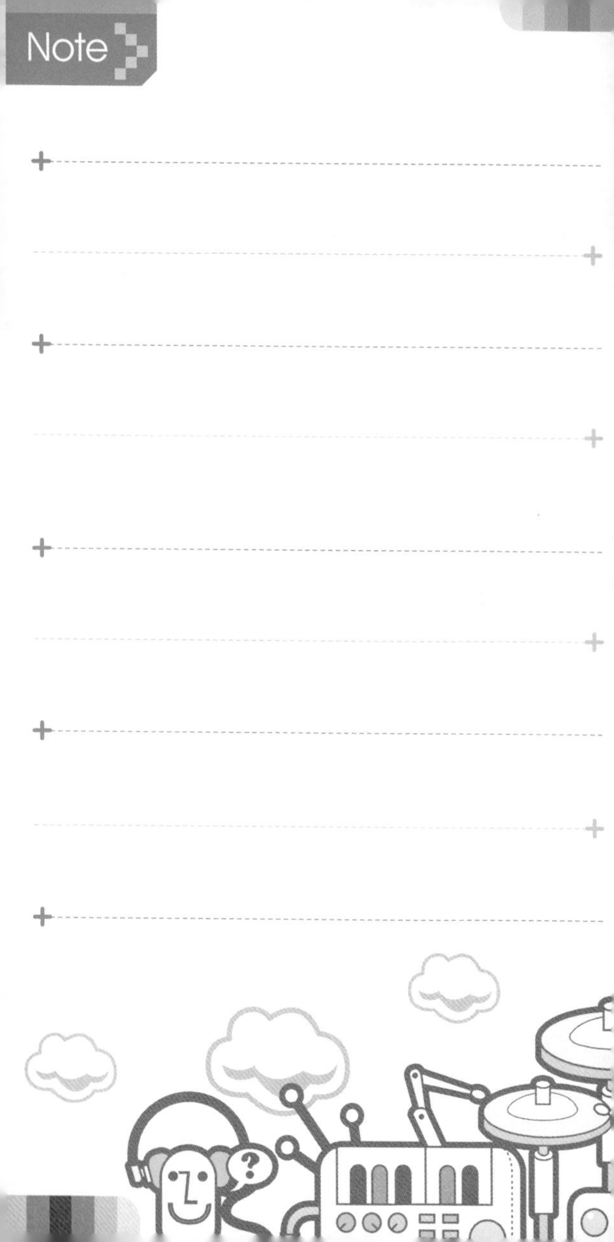
Note

Contents / 目錄

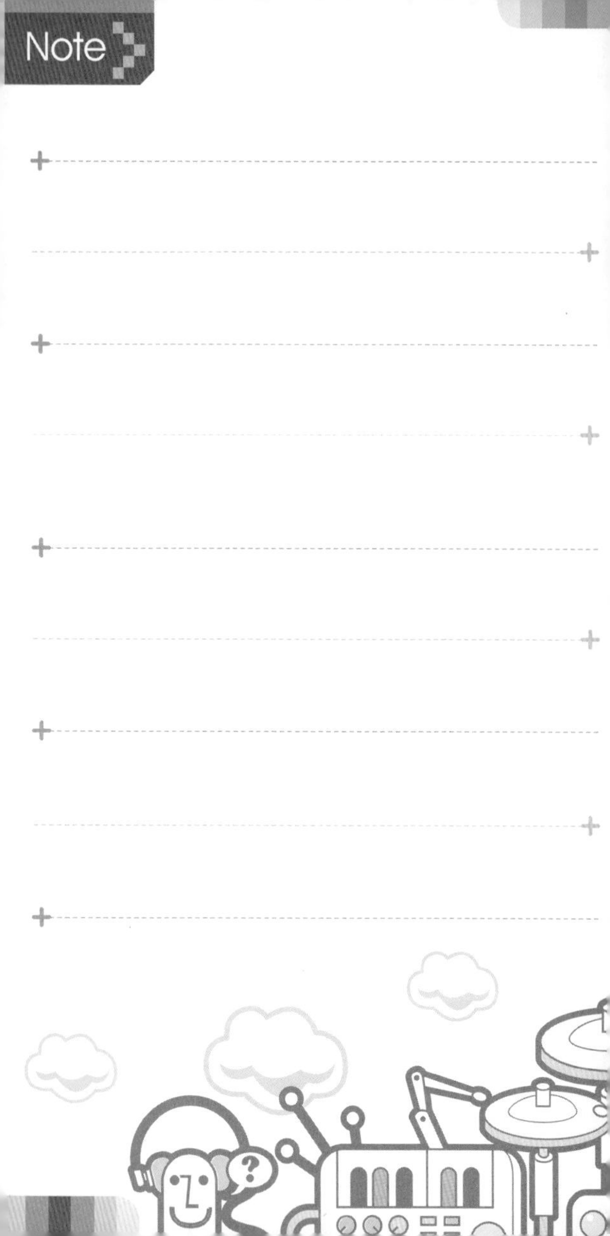
Note

01 / 新多益必考片語列表

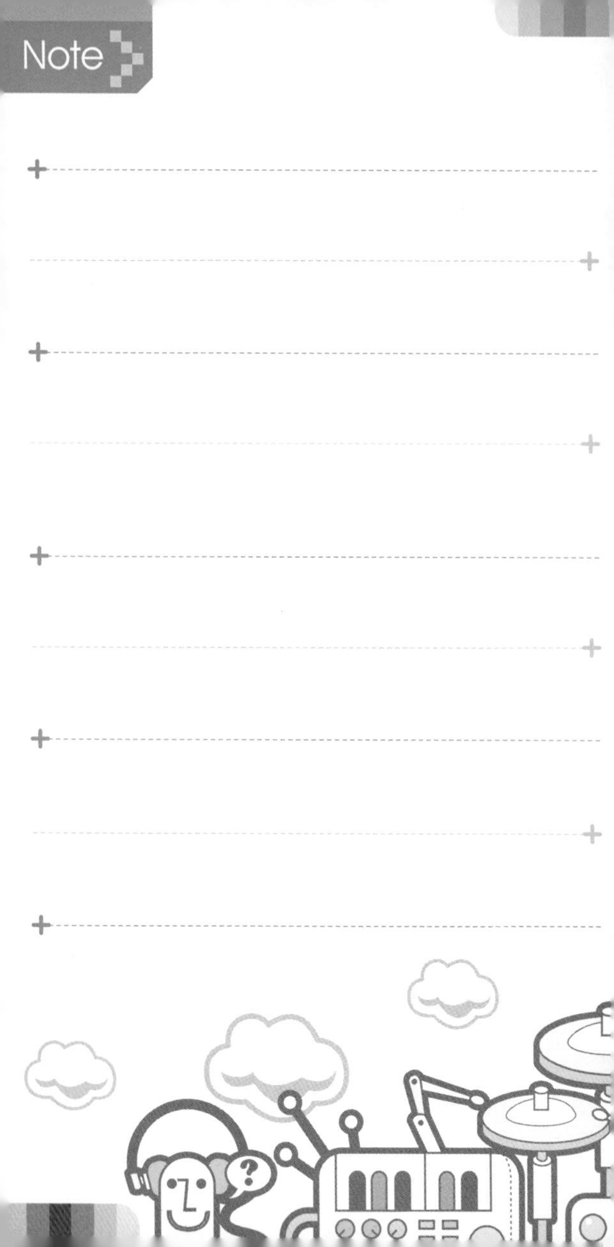
Note
?

a bunch of hot air 不切實際，沒有重點	On the surface it sounds like she knows what she's talking about, but in fact her ideas are all **a bunch of hot air**. 乍聽之下，她以為知道自己在說什麼，但其實根本沒有重點。
a clean slate 重新開始	Since bickering is pointless, I'm willing to let bygones be bygones and start with **a clean slate**. 既然爭吵毫無意義，我願意不計前嫌重新開始。
a lot riding on (sth) 仰賴我們	A lot of important buyers will attend the exhibition, so there's **a lot riding on** our ability to put our best food forward. 有很多重要的買家會參加這個展覽，所以把最好的食物端上桌要靠我們了。
a mountain of (sth) 很多的	If you spill the beans to Jean about what her sister is up to, you'll have **a mountain of** trouble on your hands. 如果你讓琴知道她姊姊的計畫，你會有大麻煩。
a windfall in 意外之財	Due to Ken's savvy investments in the stock market, he was able to enjoy **a** massive **windfall in** profits. 因為肯在股市裡很純熟的投資，他就可以享受到不小的意外之財。
all out 無保留的	John and Mary may seem like they're just having a loud discussion, but they're really having an **all out** fight. 約翰跟瑪莉似乎爭論得很大聲，不過他們真的是吵起來了。

along the same lines 同樣的內容論點	I agree in principle with your theory, but **along the same lines** it could be used against you by atheists. 我大致同意你的理論，但同時無神論者也可以以此論點推翻你。
and presto 絕對成功	Go to your lessons regularly and practice eight hours a day, **and presto**—you'll be playing like Jimi Hendrix in no time. 規律地上每一堂課，而且每天練習八小時絕對有效，你很快就可以像吉米漢得瑞克斯彈得一樣好。
as of late 到目前為止	**As of late** there have been numerous inquiries about our new line of products, but we've yet to make a sale. 直到目前為止，許多人詢問我們的新產品，但我們還沒開始賣。
(be) as pleased as punch 非常開心	When Doris learned that the Giants had won the World Series, she **was as pleased as punch**. 當陶樂絲知道巨人隊贏得世界比賽時，她非常開心。
at the risk of sounding 冒…危險	Everyone is happy about our quarterly earnings, but **at the risk of sounding** pessimistic, I'm worried that sales will drop. 大家對我們的季營收都很開心，但是也許太過悲觀，我很擔心銷售量會在近期下滑。
bail out 紓困	Many people think that the government's decision to **bail out** the auto industry was a big mistake. 很多人認為政府對汽車業紓困的決定是一大錯誤。

balance sheet 損益平衡表	At the close of this particular accounting period, I'm happy that our **balance sheet** looks good and there's an actual profit. 在這個會計年度結束之際，我很高興看到損益平衡表看來不錯，而且可以預期未來營收會提高。
bang for the buck 回收	It's natural that investors want to get as much **bang for the buck** as they can, so it's important to keep informed of market trends. 投資者希望能夠回本是理所當然的，所以了解市場狀況這件事情很重要。
bank on 依賴，信賴	Once that market opens up, we're all going to make a fortune—you can **bank on** it. 那個市場一開，我們將大賺一筆，你可以相信它的。
beat (someone) at (sb's) own game 以其人之道還治其人之身	My greatest fear is that if I reveal my ideas, someone will eventually **beat me at my own game**. 我最怕的是，如果我說了我的想法，有人會用它來對付我。
before (time) is out 在…結束前	My term paper is due next Monday, so I've got to get cracking with it this weekend **before time is out**. 我的期末報告下週一要交，所以在期限前的這個週末，我要努力將它完成。
bend to the will 態度向…傾斜	It's very stressful trying to **bend to the will** of Mrs. Grindy at every turn because she has no clue about what's going on. 由於葛蘭迪女士對發生什麼事一無所知，所以在每一個狀況發生時，要影響她的態度真的壓力很大。

be tickled pink 逗得開心	When you remembered my birthday and sent me flowers, I **was tickled pink**. 你記得我的生日，並送我花，真的讓我開心極了。
be up to (sb's) ears in (sth) 深陷於…中	Ever since I got promoted to manager I've **been up to my ears in** requests from people I don't even know. 自從我被升職為經理後，一直有一些我甚至不認識的人來要求幫忙。
big time 成功的	When I knew Mike in college he was a real goof-off, but now I hear he's hit the **big time** as a famous lawyer. 當我在大學認識麥克時，他真是成天遊手好閒，但現在他可是成功且知名的律師。
black and white 明確的定律	I'm sorry, the details of the insurance policy are spelled out in **black and white**; you won't receive any compensation. 很抱歉，保險單寫得很清楚，你將不會收到任何的賠償。
bottom line 底限	The **bottom line** is you revealed company secrets to the competition and that's why I have to let you go. 你洩露公司機密給對手，這是我們無法忍受的，所以我必須解僱你。
brace...for 防備	With the uncertainty of future energy supplies, consumers should **brace** themselves **for** any major increases in energy prices. 由於未來資源供給的不確定性，消費者應該要對能源價格的大幅上漲有防備。

break the backs of 打擊	The new government has vowed to **break the backs of** corrupt politicians who have been taking bribes for years. 新政府承諾會對付多年來收賄的腐敗政客。
break the glass ceiling 打破女性職業的藩籬	More and more women are finding ways to **break the glass ceiling** in companies and climb the corporate ladder. 越來越多女性在職場上打破藩籬成為主管。
bring forth 帶出來，激發出	The president's announcement of the new agricultural policy **brought forth** major opposition from farmers. 總統宣告新的農業政策，激發農民極大的反對聲浪。
bringing (someone) on board 引介進入	Due to irregularities in this company's accounting procedures, a new trouble-shooter has been **brought on board**. 因為這家公司的會計程序出現不正常，一位新的解決問題專家被請來公司。
building block 建築材料	Just like cells are the **building blocks** of the body, so are the citizens of this great country. 就像細胞是構成身體的原料，人民和這個大國的關係也是一樣。
(be) bummed out 洩氣	Cindy **was** all **bummed out** yesterday because she found out the guy she wants to date has turned out gay. 辛蒂昨天好洩氣，因為她想要約的男生竟然是同性戀。

(sb) can't stress (sth) enough 不能再更強調了	Your opponent will be able to spot your weaknesses quickly, so I **can't stress enough** the need to practice more. 你的對手可以很輕易地找到你的弱點，所以我必須非常強調，你需要多練習。
carbon footprint 碳足跡	Despite his riding a bicycle to work, Bill's **carbon footprint** is still large because of his many airplane trips abroad. 儘管騎腳踏車上班，比爾的碳足跡仍然很高，因為他搭機出國頻繁。
(name) carry a lot of weight 很有影響力	Just because his father is a celebrity, John's family name **carries a lot of weight** in this company. 只因為他的父親是名人，約翰的家族名號幫了這間公司不少忙。
cash in on 利用賺錢	We hope to produce our own line of smart phones to **cash in on** the world-wide craze for such devices. 我們希望有自己的智慧型手機生產線，才能在全世界瘋這款手機時賺到錢。
cash out 領出，兌現	I really need some cold hard cash right now, so I plan to **cash out** my refinance loan as soon as possible. 我真的需要點現金，所以我決定要盡快申請一些再融資貸款。
catch (sb's) breath 喘口氣	Will you slow down for just a minute? I need to **catch my breath** before we run another mile. 你可以慢一點嗎？在我們再跑一哩之前，我需要先喘口氣。

catch up on 趕上	Since I've been away for so long, I need to **catch up on** all that's been happening in the news lately. 由於我離開好一段時間，我必須要趕上最近發生的一切事情。
check out 查閱，了解	Have you **checked out** the recent corporate report? It's atrocious and the stockholders aren't happy. 你有查閱一下最近的公司報表嗎？情況並不妙，股東們不太高興。
chip in 分擔	For all that Terri has done for us over the years, we've decided to all **chip in** and get her a new computer. 基於泰瑞這麼多年來為我們所做的事，我們一起分擔幫她買一臺電腦。
clean out of 用完了	We're **clean out of** eggs; you'd better get to the supermarket and buy a couple dozen more. 我們沒有雞蛋了，你最好去超市多買幾打回來。
clear sailing ahead 前途無礙	Even though it looks like **clear sailing ahead** for the company, I still think we should prepare for a rainy day. 即使公司看來前途無礙，我還是認為我們要未雨綢繆，小心行事。
come into 得到	When Lester's grandfather died, he **came into** not only a large inheritance, but he also got all his leather clothing stores. 賴司特的祖父過世時，他不只得到大筆遺產，還繼承老人家的皮衣連鎖店。

contend with 應付	With all this competition for jobs I have to **contend with**, I seriously doubt I'll be able to find a decent job. 擁有這麼多必須應付的職場競爭，我真的懷疑我可以很快找到個好工作。
contingent on 視…情況而定	The success of this project is entirely **contingent on** whether we can get that letter of credit approved. 這個計畫成功與否，端賴於我們是否可以取得信用狀。
cool head 冷靜	Because of his ability to keep a **cool head** and work well under pressure, he's been given more responsibility. 因為他頭腦冷靜，而且可以在壓力下正常工作，所以他被賦予比較多的責任。
cost-cutting measures 降低成本的方法	Hopefully the new **cost-cutting measures** won't involve any of us, or worse yet, we'll get fired. 希望新的成本降低方案不會影響到我們，或者更糟的是，解僱我們。
decidedly for 堅決的	Sara wants to live her life **decidedly for** helping the poor instead of working for personal financial gain. 莎拉決定要以幫助窮人，而不以個人的經濟收入為主。
down-and-out 窮困潦倒的	I had lots of friends when I was living high off the hog, but now that I'm **down-and-out** nobody stays around me. 我生活優渥時有很多朋友，但我現在窮困潦倒，沒有人肯理我了。

doze off 打瞌睡	Eve keeps **dozing off** at her desk; it's a wonder she hasn't gotten fired yet. 伊芙不斷地在辦公桌前打瞌睡，奇怪的是，她竟還沒被解僱。
dress code 服裝規定	Despite the fact that our company's **dress code** isn't particularly strict, our employees still dress quite professionally. 即使我們公司的服裝規定並不特別嚴格，員工們還是穿得很專業。
easy come, easy go 來得快，去得快	Mrs. Schroeder goes on huge shopping sprees almost every day. To her, money is **easy come, easy go**. 施羅德太太每天都有大筆金額的購物。對她而言，金錢是來得快也去得快。
economic climate 經濟景氣狀況	A healthy **economic climate** can work wonders for people involved in all sectors of society, including beggars. 一個健全的經濟狀況可以讓所有階層的人創造奇蹟，甚至於乞丐呢！
emerging markets 新興市場	The key to success in this business is to identify and dominate all **emerging markets** before the competition does. 這筆生意成功的關鍵是要比競爭者先確認且主導新興市場。
experience under (sb's) belt 經驗	Some companies prefer hiring people fresh out of college, but I think having **experience under one's belt** matters. 有些公司喜歡聘請剛出校門的年輕人，可是我覺得有經驗還是很重要的。

facial gesture 臉部表情	One of the reasons I enjoy Chinese opera so much is the actors' ability to use **facial gestures** to convey different emotions. 我喜歡國劇的原因之一是演員們可以用不同的表情來詮釋不同的情緒。
financial arm 財務部門	There has been significant streamlining in the **financial arm** of the company, so I think we've started to turn a profit. 公司財務部門十分有效率，因此我覺得我們開始有盈餘了。
first thing 第一件做的事	Because my day is so unpredictable, I've decided to exercise every day **first thing** in the morning. 因為我每天的狀況不定，所以我決定每天早上第一件事就是去運動。
fly off the shelves 創造銷售佳績	Originally I had my doubts that our new product would sell, but it's actually **flying off the shelves**. 一開始我還懷疑我們的新產品會不會賣，但它的確創造了銷售佳績。
for starters 首先	What's wrong with you? **For starters** you're almost never on time and what's more, you refuse to work overtime. 你怎麼了？首先，你幾乎從不準時上班，更糟的是，你拒絕加班。
for the time being 目前，暫時	The market right now is extremely hard to predict, so I suggest that we play it conservatively **for the time being**. 現在的市場很難預測，所以我建議我們目前保守一點。

(be) geared to 配合	This new sports car **is geared to** urban professionals with plenty of money to burn. 這款新型跑車的主要訴求對象是荷包滿滿的都會專業人士。
get (someone) up to speed 讓(某人)了解	Can you **get me up to speed** on what's been happening while I was sunning myself on the beaches of Acapulco? 你可以讓我知道，在我去阿可波可度假時發生了些什麼事嗎？
get (sth) ironed out 解決	Now's the time for all of us to **get** our problems **ironed out** so that we can begin to live as brothers. 是時候我們該消除彼此的問題了，這樣我們才能開始像兄弟一樣相處。
get down to brass tacks 言歸正傳	It's fun chatting with you like this, but it's time now to **get down to brass tacks** and discuss the matter at hand. 像這樣跟你聊天真有趣，不過現在言歸正傳，該是討論正事的時候了。
get off the ground 實行	Back in high school I tried to form a band with some of my buddies, but unfortunately the project never **got off the ground**. 高中時我試過和幾個朋友組團，但很不幸，我們這個想法沒有實行。
get one's ducks in a row 條理分明	The opposition party is always against the ruling party, but they never **get their ducks in a row** and tell us exactly what they would do. 反對黨反對執政黨的一切作為，但他們從來不會條理分明地告訴我們他們到底會怎麼做。

get this sorted out 弄清楚	I'm sure we'll **get this** mess all **sorted out** by Friday so that you can enjoy your weekend without any worry. 我確定我們可以把這些問題在週五前就弄清楚，這樣你就可以不用擔心，好好地享受週末了。
get to the bottom of (sth) 追根究柢	Inner-city schools have continuously lagged behind those in more affluent areas, and we should **get to the bottom of** this problem. 貧民區的學校一直大幅落後富裕地區的學校，現在我們應該追根究柢找出問題了。
get together 聚會	All our classmates are planning on **getting together** this weekend at the Marriot Hotel. Can you come? 我們所有同學打算週末在馬力耶飯店聚會，你能來嗎？
go the extra mile 多盡一些力	That store's employees really **go the extra mile** to help their employer—no wonder their business is so good. 這間店的員工為了幫助老闆而多盡很多力，難怪生意這麼好。
go with 配合，搭配	That polka-dot shirt doesn't **go** well **with** your plain pants—I suggest something with stripes instead. 那件圓點襯衫跟你的素色長褲不搭，我建議換件條狀的吧。
goof off 偷懶	We run a very professional company here, so it goes without saying that **goofing off** on the job will not be tolerated. 我們這個公司是很專業的，所以在工作上偷懶是不可容忍的。

greeback 美鈔	With all the budget deficits, unemployment, and the real-estate crisis, the **greenback** has taken a real beating in the last couple of years. 因為預算赤字、失業率，還有房地產危機，美金在最近幾年明顯貶值。
hands-on 實際操作	It is useful to do a lot of reading on the subject, but nothing beats real **hands-on** experience to truly understand how it works. 學科的閱讀很重要，但是要真正了解實際運作，沒有什麼比實作經驗更重要了。
hang (someone) out to dry 讓(某人)身陷危險或麻煩	Paul was really **hung out to dry** when Sheila revealed his secret plan to discredit Lionel. 在席拉把保羅的祕密透露給萊諾時，他就身陷危險了。
hard cash 現金	Your credit history leaves much to be desired, so without **hard cash** up front there's really nothing I can do to help you. 你的信用紀錄不盡理想，所以如果沒有現金預先存入，我無法幫你。
have it one's way 照自己意思做	Neil was prepared to argue with Yvonne till hell froze over, but in the end he decided to just let her **have it her way**. 尼爾本來準備要跟宜芳長期爭辯，但終究還是隨她的意思。
hold a grudge 懷恨在心	What happened between Alex and I is all water under the bridge now. I no longer **hold a grudge** against him. 艾力克斯和我之間發生的事已經過去了。我對他已經不再懷恨。

hold in high esteem 備受尊崇	Many of my classmates thought that Mr. Baxter was a tyrant as a teacher, but I happen to **hold** him **in high esteem**. 我的很多同學覺得貝克司特老師是位專制的老師，不過我對他則是非常地尊崇。
hold your horses 慢點	Hey, what's your rush? You'll get your chance in due time, **hold your horses**! 喂！你在急什麼？你趕得上的，慢一點吧！
hostile takeover 惡意接收企業	The employees and the stockholders would much prefer a friendly merger as opposed to a **hostile takeover**. 職員和股東們會比較希望這是個善意的合併，而非惡意的收購。
hovering around 上下震盪	The US unemployment rate had been **hovering around** 5% for most of the decade until there was a sharp increase toward the end. 美國的失業率過去十年都在百分之五上下遊走，直到最後才有很劇烈的爬升。
in a [the] capacity 能力	This position requires an MBA degree, as well as at least two years experience **in the capacity** of manager. 這個職位要有企管碩士學歷，還要至少兩年經理的經驗。
in conjunction with 合作，結合	This series of programs is being presented **in conjunction with** the Departments of Culture and Arts. 這一連串的計畫是藝術與文化兩個部門一起呈現的。

in full swing 熱烈進行，激戰	I was worried I would arrive too early for Helen's party, but by the time I got there it was already **in full swing**. 我擔心太早到海倫的派對，可是我到場時，派對已經在熱烈進行了。
in jeopardy 危及，有危險	Christine's reckless insider trading will put our entire company **in jeopardy** if she gets caught. 克莉絲汀大膽的內線交易如果被抓到，是會危及全公司的。
in light of 藉由…影響	**In light of** the recent economic downturn, I'm afraid that there will be no year-end party and even no year-end bonuses. 因為近期的經濟衰弱，我擔心今年會沒有尾牙宴，更別提年終獎金了。
in the balance 懸而未決，成敗不定	With global warming, the earth's ecology is really **in the balance** now and the scale could tip either way. 在全球暖化的情況下，地球的生態會如何還不得而知，好、壞都有可能。
in the wings 在會議室旁的會客室	I did see Mr. Bartlette around here this morning, so he must be waiting **in the wings**. 我今天早上的確在這裡看到巴列特先生，他一定是在會客室裡等。
isn't (one's) forte 非(某人的)專長或領域	I appreciate your confidence in my Chinese ability, but translation **isn't my forte**—you should ask Mike. 我很感激你對我的中文能力有信心，可是翻譯不是我的專長，你最好請麥克幫你。

jump start 快速展開	Such a large infusion of capital was really a **jump start** for this venture; it never would have gotten off the ground without it. 這麼龐大的資金注入對於這個公司真的是很大的幫助，如果沒有它，業務真的無法起飛。
keep (someone) abreast of 讓(某人)知悉	Due to my father's illness I can't attend the conference, so please **keep me abreast of** what happens there. 因為我父親生病，我無法參加會議，所以請讓我知道會議內容。
keep (someone) posted 讓(某人)知道最新消息	While I'm away on vacation to Bali, I hope you can **keep me posted** on all the office gossip. 當我在峇里島度假時，我希望你隨時讓我知道辦公室的八卦。
kick off 展開	We're going to **kick off** this year's Pork Days celebration with a colorful parade down Main Street. 我們今年會以在緬因街的炫目遊行來展開今年的豬肉日慶典。
kick the bucket 死亡	The experimental treatment the doctor used on Dan's cancer was a success; otherwise he was surely going to **kick the bucket**. 醫生用在丹的腫瘤上的試驗治療成功了，要不然他就沒救了。
last minute 最後一刻	You've been keeping me in the dark too long—I want a detailed plan right now instead of waiting for the **last minute**. 你一直瞞著我很久了，我現在就要知道詳情而不要等到最後一刻。

last-ditch 最後一搏	With only three seconds left in the game, Terrence's shot from the far end of the court was a **last-ditch** effort to win the game. 就在比賽剩最後三秒鐘的時候，泰倫斯的遠射進球是最後贏球的關鍵。
last-gasp 苟延殘喘，纏鬥	The team was firmly ahead the whole game, so there was no need for **last-gasp** heroics toward the end. 這個球隊已經明顯領先了，所以結束前不會需要英雄式的搏命演出了。
lay the foundation 建立基礎	A reasonable understanding of grammar helps **lay the foundation** for eventual fluency in a particular foreign language. 一定程度的文法認識可以替後來的外語學習打下基礎。
leave off the table 忽略，跳過	Your idea is a good one, but you have **left** every consideration for its impact on the environment completely **off the table**. 你的主意很好，但是你忽略了所有它對環境可能發生的影響。
live high off the hog 過奢侈的生活	Because real-estate prices surged so quickly, a lot of people found themselves going from living fairly modestly to **living high off the hog** overnight. 因為房地產價格快速成長，很多人一夕之間從平凡生活過到奢華生活。
look at (someone) funny 以奇怪眼光看人	I didn't think anything was wrong until Jenny **looked at me funny** and then I realized something was amiss. 當珍妮用奇怪的眼光看我時，我不認為有什麼問題，後來我才發現有些不對勁。

lose sight of 忽略	There are a lot of distractions in college like socializing, but don't **lose sight of** your academic goals. 在大學裡有很多讓人分心的事，如交際等，可是不要讓學術目標失焦。
lowest [highest] rungs of 最低[最高]階層	Unskilled and uneducated workers occupy the **lowest rungs of** the societal ladder, with very few opportunities to climb up. 缺乏技能和沒受教育的工作者位居社會底層，而且很少有機會晉升。
make hay while the sun shines 打鐵趁熱，把握時機	It's all so easy to relax and rest on our laurels, but I think we should continue to work hard and **make hay while the sun shines**. 放輕鬆且安於現狀很容易，可是我覺得我們應該繼續努力，把握時機。
market is saturated 市場飽和	Your idea is all nice and good, but you seem to have forgotten that the **market is saturated** with smart phones now. 你的主意很棒，可是你好像忘記了市場上的智慧手機已經飽和了。
mess up 搞砸	The arguments you made in your paper were very convincing, but unfortunately you totally **messed up** your bibliography. 雖然你作業裡提出的論點很具說服力，但很可惜，你的參考書目卻做得亂七八糟。
mind your Ps and Qs 注意言行	That's a very conservative company, so if you're going to work there you need to **mind your Ps and Qs** and behave yourself. 那是間很保守的公司，所以如果你要在那裡工作，你必須注意言行，而且行為得宜。

more than welcome 敬請	For all that you've done for me, you're **more than welcome** to stop by and visit anytime you like. 為了感謝你為我所做的一切，我歡迎你隨時來作客。
move up the corporate ladder 升職	I used to be ambitious and only wanted to **move up the corporate ladder**, but now I'm totally content. 我曾經非常有企圖心，只想在公司裡升職，但是現在我很知足。
null and void 無效的	The contract was finally made **null and void** and all parties involved went their separate ways. 這個合約最終無效，而參與者都各自發展了。
off-putting 令人煩惱的，惱人的	Most of us are sick and tired of Stan's **off-putting** attitude and we're planning on confronting him with it. 我們大部分人都受不了史丹惱人的態度，我們計畫要跟他當面解決。
off the charts 破表	The CEO is elated that the recent sales figures are **off the charts**, but he's puzzled as why things have improved so much. 近來銷售數字破表，執行長很高興，不過他對進步這麼多的原因感到很困惑。
(person) of means 有手段的人	The founder and president of that company wasn't always **a man of means**; he started out as a poor peasant boy. 這間公司的創辦人，也是總裁，並非一直是個有手段的人，他一開始只是個窮困的農家男孩。

on [at] an even keel 穩定	Some people like to take chances, but I'm more conservative and prefer to keep things **at an even keel**. 有些人喜歡冒險，可是我比較保守，喜歡所有事情都是穩定的。
on the eve of 即將發生	Do you think we're **on the eve of** interstellar travel, or are we destined to be stuck on this rock until the end of time? 你認為我們即將有機會展開星際旅遊，還是我們注定只能在這個星球上了？
on the fritz 壞掉了	The bargain-priced computer does have its drawbacks—it's almost always **on the fritz**. 這個便宜的電腦的確有它的缺點，它幾乎經常當機。
once and for all 一勞永逸	This problem has plagued us for far too long—it's time we got to the root of it and eradicated it **once and for all**. 這個問題影響我們已經太久了，是時候我們該找到根源一勞永逸地解決它了。
open the floor up to 開放現場	That's about all I have to say for now, so I'd like to **open the floor up to** a question-and-answer period now. 以上就是我所要說的，現在我想開放現場進行提問。
paring down 減少	We've decided that **paring down** the company will make it more streamlined, and some of you will get sacked. 我們決定將公司規模縮小，讓它更有效率，你們有些人會被解僱。

pay lip service to 嘴上說說而已	She's just **paying lip service to** him by saying that she'll help him out; she's not going to lift one finger! 她跟他說會幫忙只是說說而已，她才不會真的做呢！
people in high places 上流階層	I'm normally a fairly anti-social person, but I'll be outgoing if it means meeting **people in high places**. 我是個蠻反社會的人，但我從不會因為認識上流階層的人而興奮。
pour money into 資金挹注	The government's policy of **pouring money into** the military makes the conservatives happy, but the liberals are of course upset. 政府挹注軍隊資金讓保守派很開心，不過自由派當然就不高興了。
precious little 非常地少	There's **precious little** time to get the project done, so you'd better get your butt in gear! 只剩極少時間可以來完成任務，你們最好馬上行動。
prepared statement 準備好的聲明	In a **prepared statement**, the president outlined what he feels the necessary steps we need to take to get the economy rolling again. 在準備好的聲明裡，總統概述他覺得重振經濟的必要步驟。
profligate energy 浪費資源	We've been spoiled with cheap energy for so long that we've all become **profligate energy** users. 我們被廉價的資源寵壞了，以至於我們都成了浪費資源的人。

property casualty insurance 產物保險	In many respects, it's a good idea to take out **property casualty insurance** on such things as your car, home, or business. 在諸多考慮下，把一些東西如車子、房子或公司都保產物保險是不錯的想法。
pull one's weight 盡自己的本分	Colin hasn't been **pulling his weight** for some time, and I'm sick of always having to cover for him. 柯林已經很久沒有盡他的本分了，我受夠了一直幫他掩飾。
pull the plug on 取消	Because of the recent economic downturn, the government has had to **pull the plug on** many unnecessary programs. 因為最近經濟下滑，政府不得不針對一些不需要的計畫喊停。
put a strain on 造成負擔	My mother-in-law's illness and my wife's need to be her full-time caretaker have really **put a strain on** our marriage. 我岳母的病情和我太太必須成為她的全職看護這兩件事，給我們的婚姻造成負擔。
put it on (sb's) tab 記在帳上	I'm a little short of cash, bartender. Can you just **put it on my tab**? 我的現金有點不夠，酒保。你可以記在我的帳上嗎？
put it on plastic 用信用卡	Being in debt is something I've never been comfortable with, but this time I'll make an exception and **put it on plastic**. 我一直不喜歡負債，不過這次例外，我要用信用卡付款。

put together 組合	We decided to **put together** a thorough plan to eradicate all waste from the company during the coming fiscal year. 我們決定要組合出一個詳細計畫來消除公司下一個會計年度裡的浪費。
reach out to 為了…	The candidate's tour down south was nothing but an effort to **reach out to** voters for the upcoming election. 這位候選人去南部不為別的，只是為了即將到來的選舉而去接近選民。
recipe for failure 失敗的原因	Showing up for a job interview wearing jeans and a T-shirt is a **recipe for failure**. 穿著牛仔褲和T恤去面試注定要失敗。
red tape 繁瑣的文件	My new health food store would be turning a profit if it weren't for all that needless government **red tape**. 如果不是因為政府要求的繁瑣文件，我新開的健康食品店應該會很賺錢。
resign to 認命	I wanted to get a government job, but due to my lack of education I've had to **resign** myself **to** working as a cashier. 我本來希望擔任公職，但因為學歷不夠，只能認命地去當收銀員。
rock bottom 最低潮	It wasn't until she hit **rock bottom** with her alcoholism that she decided to turn her life around and clean up her act. 直到她因為酗酒而人生觸底，她才決定要徹底改變，重啟人生。

roll out
推出，上市

There can be no further delays! The new product line must be **rolled out** within this month or our company is doomed! 不能再拖了！新產品這個月一定要推出，不然公司就完蛋了。

roughly speaking
大致而言

I can't give you an exact time frame, but **roughly speaking**, I'm sure we should be able to finish the project before the end of the quarter. 我無法告訴你確定的時程，不過大致而言，我確定我們應該可以在這一季結束前完成這個案子。

round up[down]
加價[減價]

Please note that all prices have been **rounded up** to the nearest full-dollar value. 請注意，所有價格都已經加價到近乎與美金計價同值了。

sales pitch
推銷的說辭

There's no denying that your **sales pitch** is very convincing, but the bottom line is I don't need your products. 無可否認的，你的推銷十分有說服力，但重點是我不需要你的產品。

secure a loan
取得貸款

The idea to open a restaurant is a solid one, but we can't begin to make it happen until we **secure a loan** from the bank. 開餐廳是確定的了，可是我們必須要先得到銀行貸款才行。

sell like hotcakes
暢銷

Despite its massive amount of calories, the new bacon double cheeseburger has been **selling like hotcakes**. 儘管含有高量的卡路里，這種新的培根雙層吉士堡還是大受歡迎。

settle upon 在…完成	Masie wanted to have her wedding in June, but because of her mother's illness she had to **settle upon** May. 瑪西想要在六月結婚，可是因為她母親的病，她必須在五月完婚。
shake (sth) up 整頓，使更好	The board of directors decided to **shake** things **up** in the company by threatening to reduce year-end bonuses. 董事會威脅降低年終獎金，以示整頓公司的決心。
shake up 震盪，影響	The loss of the Cosby account is going to cause a big **shake up** in the company. I fear I may get demoted. 失去寇斯比這個客戶將對公司造成很大的影響，我擔心我會被降職。
shore up 穩住	We need to **shore up** some support for Carlos as he's been going through a real tough time recently. 卡羅斯最近日子很煎熬，我們需要給他更多穩定的支持。
simply put 簡而言之	There is a lot to say about Jake's speech, but **simply put**, it was amazing. 傑克的演講真的可圈可點，簡言之，就是真的太棒了。
slide into 滑進，駛進	Just before I was about to park, some idiot **slid into** the spot that I was going to take. 就在我正要停車時，某個白目的傢伙竟然停進了我的位子。

slip under the radar 不要被發現，維持低調	Hackers have become so skillful now that even the best anti-virus programs can't stop viruses from **slipping under their radar**. 近年來，駭客的技巧越來越高明，即使最棒的防毒程式都無法防堵最新的病毒偷偷入侵。
slug it out 纏鬥	I say we let the two of them settle their differences by **slugging it out** rather than having them get useless counseling. 我建議讓他們兩個自己花時間去解決爭議，別浪費時間在無用的諮商上了。
snatch up 奪走	Peter's been **snatching up** all sorts of cheap houses in the low-rent district, hoping to fix them up and sell them for a profit. 彼得收購低租金地區的便宜房子，希望把它們修理之後賣了賺錢。
soften the blow 降低影響	I not only lost my job which I had held for the past 20 years, but I have no savings to help **soften the blow**. 我不只失去了做了二十年的工作，還沒有任何存款可以讓影響小一點。
spar with 爭辯	With the massive amounts of experience you have, I know better than to **spar with** the likes of you. 基於你的豐富經驗，我非常清楚，不要跟你這樣的人爭辯。
spare no expense 不惜代價	The committee is fully committed to making this amusement park a success—they've **spared no expense**. 這個委員會承諾要讓這間遊樂園成功，他們不惜代價都要做到。

spick and span 一塵不染	If I don't see this place **spick and span** within an hour, you'll all be given your walking papers! 如果我一小時之內沒有看到這裡一塵不染，我就叫你滾。
squeeze out 解僱	Some employees were **squeezed out** by the recent economic downturn, and won't be rehired even if things get better. 一些員工因為近期經濟衰退而被解僱，而且即使經濟好轉，他們也不會被重新聘僱。
stay put 不要動	It's probably best to just **stay put** right now until the rain lets up. 在雨停之前，還是不要離開比較好。
stay the course 堅守崗位[信念]	Because Edwina was able to **stay the course** in her marriage to James, they weathered the storm and didn't get divorced. 因為愛得溫娜在與詹姆士的婚姻裡堅持信念，他們克服困難且沒有離婚。
stock up 囤積	He's so paranoid that he **stocks up** on canned food in case some kind of terrible natural disaster might strike. 他很偏執，所以囤積了很多罐頭食品，以備某些天災發生之需。
strike a balance 設法達到平衡	I've really taken to being a father, but it's often difficult to **strike a** healthy **balance** between my career and family. 我很認真地想做個好父親，可是要在工作和家庭間達到平衡很困難。

strike up old acquaint-ances 重拾友誼	I **struck up** a lot of **old acquaintances** at my last class reunion, though I still thought it was a rather boring affair. 我在上次同學會重拾了好多友誼，雖然我覺得很無聊。
subprime mortgage crisis 次級房貸風暴	Everything was really peachy until the hated **subprime mortgage crisis** hit, putting us all in the welfare line. 直到次貸風暴發生之前，一切看來十分美好，而我們現在都在領救濟金了。
suit one's fancy 投某人所好	I'm a huge opera fan, and being able to see Aida performed at the Lincoln Center would really **suit my fancy**. 我是個歌劇迷，能夠在林肯中心看「阿依達」這齣歌劇的演出，我會很高興。
sure-fire 必定成功的	I've heard that one **sure-fire** way to get your videos noticed on YouTube is to make yourself look as stupid as possible. 我聽說要讓你的影片在YouTube受到矚目必定成功的唯一方法，就是讓你自己看來蠢到不能再蠢。
take a lot of blows 受創多次	The coach **took a lot of blows** from the public when he announced the new player's massive salary. 在教練公布新球員鉅額的薪資時，他飽受大眾不斷地攻擊。
take measures 利用方法	Due to our magazine's recent loss of subscribers, the following **measures** will be **taken** to turn things around. 因為最近雜誌訂戶減少，要施行下面的方法來讓狀況反轉。

take the helm 接班，主導	There is great anxiety amongst the staff about what will happen should the CEO's inept son **take the helm** of the company. 萬一執行長無能的兒子接班會發生什麼事，大家都很心急想知道。
talk (some-one) into (anything) 說服	I will never let you **talk me into** accepting that nightmare assignment. Why don't you just take no for an answer? 我絕對不會讓你說服我去接那份恐怖的工作。你為什麼不能接受事實呢？
tap for 隨手可得	Because of the abundant coastline of Taiwan, many people feel the tides could be easily **tapped for** clean and cheap energy. 因為臺灣資源豐富的海岸線，人們覺得潮水可以輕易帶來乾淨且便宜的資源。
teeter on the edge 在邊緣遊走	That building was built right along a fault line; it's **teetering on the edge** of disaster. 這個建築物建在不正確的位置上，它隨時都可能有危險的。
that's it for 就這些了，結束了	**That's it for** our program today, please join us again next time for another edition of *What's New in Taipei.* See ya! 這就是我們今天的節目，下次請參與我們另一個節目『臺北新鮮事』的播出。下回見。
the here and now 眼前	There's no reason to argue about the mistakes of the past; I prefer to deal with what faces us in **the here and now**. 沒有道理為了過去的錯誤爭執，我覺得要解決眼前的問題才是。

the ins and outs 詳細情形	I have no practical business background, I'm hoping you could show me **the ins and outs** of running a small business. 沒有特別的商業背景，我希望你可以讓我知道你對於經營小生意的詳細計畫。
the picture of sth 現象，狀況	Eleanor is **the picture of** dedication; I've never seen someone keep trying so hard despite the small chance of succeeding. 愛蓮娜是個專注的好榜樣。我從來沒看過一個人在希望如此渺茫的狀況下仍然努力嘗試。
there's a catch 有問題	It's a pretty good deal on the surface, but **there is a catch**－you have to sign the contract for a two-year period. 表面上看起來這是個好交易，可是其實是有問題的，你必須要簽兩年的合約。
thick skin 厚臉皮	Brenda has such **thick skin** that I'm about ready to tear my hair out after trying to negotiate with her. 布蘭達厚臉皮到我跟她周旋後幾乎要扯下我的頭髮(很傷腦筋之意)。
throw in the towel 認輸	I appreciate your efforts in trying to make this project work, but it has failed and it's time to **throw in the towel**. 感謝你們真的很用心想讓這個案子成功，可是很明顯失敗了，該是時候認輸了。
tighten (sb's) belt 減少開支，勒緊褲帶	No one seems to understand that even the government has to **tighten its belt** during lean economic times. 似乎無人了解，在經濟不佳時，即使是政府也要減少開支。

tough luck 不走運	Tracy has had some **tough luck** of late with various setbacks in her job, not to mention a rather unstable family life. 崔西最近在工作上不太順利，更別提她最近家庭生活也不太好。
under wraps 保密，封鎖	Roger is furious with you for letting the cat out of the bag! The new marketing plan was supposed to stay **under wraps**. 羅傑因為你的洩密對你很生氣。這個新的行銷策略應該要保密的。
up (one's) sleeve 打什麼主意	Phil seems trustworthy, but I'm always suspicious that he's got something sneaky **up his sleeve**. 表面看來菲爾很值得信任，但我總覺得他在打些什麼主意。
up the ante 有助益	Our risky decision to **up the ante** by investing in the semi-conductor industry years ago really paid off. 我們多年前冒險的決定以投資半導體產業來增加收益，真的值回票價了。
up the creek without a paddle 糟糕了	You might have to swallow your pride and take my suggestion; otherwise you're surely going to be **up the creek without a paddle**. 你可能要收起自傲，接受建議，不然可能會有麻煩哦！
up to (sb's) eyeballs in sth 情況嚴重	I'm **up to my eyeballs in** paperwork and won't see the light at the end of the tunnel until well after Christmas. 我的工作多到可能要到聖誕節後才可以喘口氣。

up to (one's) eyes in sth 太多	I was really looking forward to our evening date, but I'm **up to my eyes in** work and won't be punching out until well after 10. 我真的很期待今晚與你共進晚餐，但是我工作實在太多，可能得加班到十點。
weather the storm 通過考驗	Because they were able to **weather the storm** of last year's recession so well, that company made a fortune while their competitions went bankrupt. 因為這公司去年妥善地因應不景氣，其他競爭者倒閉時他們卻賺錢。
weighed down 頹喪，低迷	The failure of the soccer league was inevitable as despite healthy ticket sales, it was **weighed down** by huge player salaries. 足球聯盟的失敗是無可避免的，雖然票賣得不錯，但聯盟因球員的高薪而經營不振。
withstand wear and tear 禁得起考驗	I used to buy all my clothes at the night market, but now I prefer spending more on clothes that will **withstand wear and tear**. 我以前都是在夜市買衣服，但現在我會花多點錢買比較耐穿的衣服。
work the room 與人們交際應酬	I'm always amazed at how many contacts Harriet makes at these business luncheons. She really knows how to **work the room**. 我總是很驚訝於哈利葉在午餐會上能認識多少人。她真會交際應酬。

2 / 新多益必考片語問題集

Note

The generals thought they had set a convincing trap, but the enemy smelled a rat and didn't ________.

A stand above the rest

B in case of

C swallow the bait

Your proposal is very attractive, but it would bring about a major change in my life if I were to accept it—I'll need to ________ it ________ for a few days.

A hire...out

B mull...over

C dodge...for

解答 001

解答 **(C) swallow the bait 上當**

將軍們以為他們設了一個很有說服力的陷阱，可是敵人察覺出不對勁，沒上當。

選項 (A)stand above the rest 出類拔萃 (B)in case of 假如 (C)swallow the bait 上當

補充例句

- **stand above the rest 出類拔萃**

Despite Eric's diminutive stature, his persistence and unsurpassed skills have allowed him to *stand above the rest*. 雖然艾瑞克個子不高，但是他的韌性和傑出的能力讓他出類拔萃。

- **in case of 假如**

Knowing exactly what to do *in case of* an emergency could be a real lifesaver in the event of an actual disaster. 知道假如有緊急事件時該如何反應，在災難真的發生時會有救命的效果。

解答 002

解答 **(B) mull...over 詳細思考**

你的提議很吸引人，如果我接受，對我的生活會有很大影響；我需要幾天時間好好考慮。

選項 (A)hire...out 放棄原有計畫而轉為他職 (B)mull...over 詳細思考 (C)dodge...for 推託

補充例句

- **hire...out 放棄原有計畫而轉為他職**

His original idea of getting a regular job as a music teacher hasn't planned out, so he's decided to *hire* himself *out* as a musician for private parties and such. 他原本想找個固定的音樂老師的工作，但沒有成功，所以他決定放棄而轉做私人聚會的樂師。

- **dodge...for 推託**

Because their business venture provided so many new jobs to the poor village, they were able to *dodge* responsibility *for* any environmental impact. 因為他們公司提供了這貧窮村莊很多新的工作機會，所以他們可以推託對當地環境造成影響的責任。

The college entrance examination was so hard that the actual classes I took in university were ________ by comparison.

A **a ballpark figure**

B **tapped in**

C **a walk in the park**

Lisa's father is vehemently opposed to her marrying you, Dick you're fighting a[an] ________.

A **got to hand it to**

B **queue up**

C **uphill battle**

解答 003

解答 **(C) a walk in the park 簡單的事**
大學入學考非常難，比較起來，我覺得實際在大學修的課好簡單。

選項 (A)a ballpark figure 大約的數字 (B)tapped in 利用 (C)a walk in the park 簡單的事

補充例句

▸ **a ballpark figure** 大約的數字
If you can't give me exact statistics, John, can you at least give me *a ballpark figure*? I need at least something to go on. 約翰，如果你無法給我明確的統計，最起碼可以給我個大約的數字嗎？我需要這個數字做事。

▸ **tap in** 利用
The country is hoping to find vast natural resources that they can *tap in* for future economic gain. 這個國家希望找到大量的自然資源，以利用來取得未來的經濟收益。

解答 004

解答 **(C) uphill battle 情勢艱難的抗爭**
麗莎的父親非常反對她嫁給你，狄克，你在打一場很艱困的仗哦！

選項 (A)got to hand it to 必須放手給… (B)queue up 排隊 (C)uphill battle 情勢艱難的抗爭

補充例句

▸ **get to hand it to** 必須放手給…
I *got to hand it to* you, Kevin; you really know how to charm the ladies with your smooth talk and confidence. 我必須要讓你接手了，凱文，你真的比較能夠用你的溫柔語言和自信取信女性。

▸ **queue up** 排隊
Many people had *queued up* for tickets outside the box office for several hours before tickets for the concert went on sale. 在演唱會門票開賣之前，人們必須在售票亭前排隊好幾個小時。

Several sectors of the economy ________ chaos when the real-estate crisis began a few years ago.

A **plunged into**

B **took decisive action on**

C **insisted on**

Enthusiasm was feverish at the start of the campaign, but for some strange reason it had totally ________ within only a week of its launch.

A **remained afloat**

B **fallen flat**

C **stacked up**

解答 005

解答 **(A) plunged into 陷入**

當房地產危機在幾年前開始時，好幾項行業的經濟狀況都因此陷入混亂。

選項 (A)plunged into 陷入 (B)took decisive action on 具決斷力的行動 (C) insisted on 堅持

補充例句

▸ **take decisive action on 具決斷力的行動**

Perhaps the reason why so many representatives weren't re-elected in the last election is because they failed to *take decisive action on* creating jobs. 也許很多代表在上次選舉沒有被提名的原因，是因為他們在製造就業機會上沒有決斷力的行動。

▸ **insist on 堅持**

Many small stores in Taiwan still don't accept any kind of credit cards —they *insist on* hard cash instead. 很多臺灣商店還是不接受信用卡，他們堅持只收現金。

解答 006

解答 **(B) fallen flat 未達預期效果，瓦解了**

在選舉初期，民眾的熱情高漲，但因某些奇怪原因，在展開了一週內，熱情就完全冷卻了。

選項 (A)remained afloat 順利，流暢 (B)fallen flat 未達預期效果，瓦解了 (C)stacked up 優於，突出

補充例句

▸ **remain afloat 順利，流暢**

The company has *remained afloat* despite massive stockholders' sellouts earlier this year. 雖然今年年初很多大股東賣掉股票，公司營運仍然維持正常。

▸ **stack up 優於，突出**

I know you are very proud of your ideas, Ken, but they just don't *stack up* when compared to those of your colleagnes. 我知道你對你的想法很自豪，肯，可是跟你其他同事的主意比起來並不突出。

Some of the most complicated statistics and sales figures can seem like child's play ________ a qualified number cruncher.

A fit in the equation

B in shambles

C in the hands of

Mr. Edwards made the mistake of hiring a tyrannical new manager, and as a result the employees have been quitting ________ .

A in droves

B profits are squeezed

C on the whole

解答 007

解答 **(C) in the hands of 在手，拿著的**

有些非常複雜的統計和銷售數字到了會計老手的手上，彷彿成了小兒科。

選項 (A)fit in the equation 狀況中的變數 (B)in shambles 混亂與廢墟 (C)in the hands of 在手，拿著的

補充例句

- **fit in the equation 狀況中的變數**

This product is geared toward the mainstream, but I'm not sure how blacks or other minorities will *fit in the equation*. 這個產品已經逐漸成為主流商品，不過我不確定次級品或一般品在這市場中會有何影響。

- **in shambles 混亂與廢墟**

Phil's life was *in shambles* after his dad died, his wife divorced him and he was devoted to work. 菲爾的生活在他父親過世後變得混亂，他的太太和他離婚，而他只好投身工作。

解答 008

解答 **(A) in droves 成群結隊**

愛德華先生犯了個錯誤，僱用一位暴君作經理，結果他的職員集體辭職。

選項 (A)in droves 成群結隊 (B)profits are squeezed 獲利緊縮 (C)on the whole 整體而言

補充例句

- **profits are squeezed 獲利緊縮**

We have to face the fact that *profits are squeezed* due to higher production costs and dwindling sales. 我們必須面對因為高製作成本和業務量縮減而獲利緊縮的事實。

- **on the whole 整體而言**

Some departments have had to downsize for sure, but *on the whole* our number of employees has remained fairly steady. 某些部門確定要裁撤，但大體而言，我們的員工人數維持穩定。

After living on skid row ________, Jenny was finally able to afford an education and achieve a better life for herself and her family.

A make sense

B bring up the rear

C for years

Because he wants to finish his dissertation before the deadline, Daniel has ________ research for the past several weeks.

A been absent from

B been engrossed in

C been abundant in

解答 009

解答 **(C) for years 很久的時間**

在貧民區住了好幾年，珍妮終於有能力求學，並且為她和家人帶來比較好的生活。

選項 (A)make sense 合理 (B)bring up the rear 殿後，業績落後 (C)for years 很久的時間

補充例句

▸ **make sense 合理**

What Irene said at the meeting *made* the most *sense*, but the boss liked Jerry's idea better—he's such a brown-noser. 艾琳在會議中說得最合理，可是老闆比較喜歡傑瑞的說法，他真是會拍馬屁。

▸ **bring up the rear 殿後，業績落後**

It was such an embarrasement for me at the track meet—all my teammates finished toward the front while I *brought up the rear*. 賽跑的結果真令我難堪，所有的隊友都跑到終點了，只有我殿後。

解答 010

解答 **(B) been engrossed in 全神貫注於**

因為他想要在截止日前完成論文，所以丹尼爾在過去幾週裡全心投入研究。

選項 (A)been absent from 缺席，不在 (B)been engrossed in 全神貫注於 (C)been abundant in 資源豐富

補充例句

▸ **be absent from 缺席，不在**

I'm afraid Carolyn has a bit of the sniffles this morning, so she'll *be absent from* school today, Mrs. Butler. 巴特樂老師，卡洛琳今天早上有點流鼻涕，所以她今天無法來上課。

▸ **be abundant in 資源豐富**

The area along the coast *is abundant in* wildlife, so it's no wonder so many people protested the company's plan to build a refinery there. 這一區沿著海岸有豐富的自然生態，難怪很多人抗議這個公司在這裡建煉油廠的計畫。

Miss Li experienced huge culture shock when she went to study in the U.S. as she was simply not ________ the relatively open lifestyle there.

A absorbed in

B used to

C in the habit of

The lecture was very interesting at first, but one of the students' incessant comments and questions ________ the teacher's for most of it.

A abided by

B took up the attention of

C were rich in

解答 011

解答 **(B) used to 習慣於**

李小姐到美國唸書時，經歷了巨大的文化衝擊，因為她不太習慣那裡開放的生活方式。

選項 (A)absorbed in 全神貫注於 (B)used to 習慣於 (C)in the habit of 有這個習慣

補充例句

- **be absorbed in 全神貫注於**
  Lenny is very active and seldom sits still, but he's *been absorbed in* that book you bought him all morning. 藍尼很好動，很少乖乖坐著，可是他整個早上都專心看你買給他的那本書。
- **be in the habit of 有這個習慣**
  Mr. Robin *was* not *in the habit of* removing his shoes before entering someone's home, so it took him a while to adjust to the custom. 羅賓先生在進別人屋裡時沒有脫鞋的習慣，所以他花了一些時間適應。

解答 012

解答 **(B) took up the attention of 吸引…的注意**

這堂課一開始很有趣，但當中一位學生持續的批評和提問吸引了老師幾乎整堂課的注意力。

選項 (A)abided by 忠於，遵守 (B)took up the attention of 吸引…的注意 (C) were rich in 富於

補充例句

- **abide by (= be faithful to; obey) 忠於，遵守**
  You may be new here, but you are still expected to *abide by* the rules just like everybody else. 你也許初來乍到，可是你跟其他人一樣要遵守這裡的規定。
- **be rich in 富於**
  Dairy products, soy beans and fish *are* all *rich in* calcium, which is essential to having healthy and strong bones. 乳製品、豆類和魚都富含鈣質，對健康和強壯的骨骼是不可或缺的。

The terracotta warriors of Xian were discovered completely ________ when some farmers were digging a well.

A by accident

B of their own accord

C in accord with

The plan sounded too good to be true at first, but it failed to ________ the weather ________ and the sudden rainstorm ruined everything.

A take...into account

B give...an account of

C adapt...for

解答 013

解答 **(A) by accident 意外**

西安兵馬俑是一群農夫在掘井時意外發現的。

選項 (A)by accident 意外 (B)of their own accord 自願地，主動地(C)in accord with 與…一致

補充例句

▸ **of one's own accord 自願地，主動地**

No one asked Lisa to provide all that information; she did it completely *of her own accord*. 沒有人要求莉莎提供那些訊息，她完全是自願的。

▸ **in accord with 與…一致**

Because his ideas are not *in accord with* the doctrine of our church, he has been asked to stop attending services. 因為他的想法跟我們教會的教義不符，他已經被要求停止參加禮拜了。

解答 014

解答 **(A) take...into account 把…考慮進去**

這個計畫一開始聽起來好得不像真的，可是它沒把天氣考慮進去，而突來的大雨毀了一切。

選項 (A)take...into account (= consider) 把…考慮進去 (B)give...an account of 說明，解釋(理由) (C)adapt...for 改編，改寫(以適應新的需要)

補充例句

▸ **give...an account of 說明，解釋(理由)**

I put my complete trust in you, Steven, but I won't make any decisions until everyone *gives* me *an account of* what they think happened. 我完全信任你，史蒂芬，可是直到我聽過大家對事發經過的說明，我才會做決定。

▸ **adapt...for (= make sth suitable for a new need) 改編，改寫(以適應新的需要)**

Even though this mountain bicycle was designed for off-road riding, it can easily be *adapted for* use on city streets or as a touring bike. 即使這登山腳踏車是為了越野而設計的，可是它也可以很容易就適應一般市區道路或旅遊騎乘。

Most of the data is about what everyone expected, but we just can't ________ the discrepencies in one particular sector.

A be well supplied with

B account for

C accuse of

It isn't so much that I ________ Taiwanese culture, but rather that as a country boy I'm not used to living in such a large city as Taipei.

A am not accustomed to

B am not acquainted with

C am not liable for

解答 015

解答 **(B) account for 解釋，說明**

大部分的資料都如眾人預期，可是我們無法解釋在一個特別區塊的瑕疵。

選項 (A)be well supplied with 富於，富有 (B)account for (= give an explanation or reason for) 解釋，說明 (C)accuse of 指控，控告

補充例句

▸ **be well supplied with 富於，富有**

It is my opinion that our forces in the field *are* not *well supplied with* even the very basic essentials, such as weapons, ammunition and food. 我認為我軍在戰場上沒有足夠的資源，即使是最基本的必需品，譬如武器、火藥和食物。

▸ **accuse of 指控，控告**

He was *accused of* murder, found guilty, and spent 10 years in the slammer before he was exonerated by the court after DNA evidence was presented. 在DNA證據被法庭提出與被判無罪前，他被指控謀殺，被判有罪及十年的牢獄。

解答 016

解答 **(A) am not accustomed to 適應**

問題並不完全在於我不適應臺灣文化，而是身為一個鄉下小孩，我不太習慣臺北這種大都市。

選項 (A)am not accustomed to 適應 (B)am not acquainted with 熟悉 (C)am not liable for 負責

補充例句

▸ **be acquainted with 熟悉**

Having had friends from England since he was a kid, Mr. Guo *was* well *acquainted with* English culture and had no problems adjusting to life there. 郭先生自孩提時候就有來自英國的朋友，他對於英國文化很熟悉，而且適應那裡的生活完全沒有問題。

▸ **be liable for 負責**

Even though you'll be operating company vehicles, you'*re* still *liable for* any damage caused in case of accidents you cause. 即使你是開公司車，如果有任何意外發生，你還是要自己負責。

Lisa's parents were desperate to have her marry before the age of 30, but on the other hand they wouldn't just ________ any guy she chose.

A apply to

B approve of

C arise from

I know it's for the good of the company, but I ________ what will happen if Mary finds out we're all conspiring to get her fired.

A am anxious about

B am ashamed of

C am aware of

解答 017

解答 **(B) approve of 肯定，接受，允諾**

莉莎的父母急切地想要在她三十歲前把她嫁出去，可是另一方面他們又看不上她的人選。

選項 (A)apply to 與…相關，適用 (B)approve of 肯定，接受，允諾 (C)arise from 由…引起

補充例句

▸ **apply to 與…有關，適用**

Those are very important considerations I must admit, but they don't *apply to* this situation; there's no need to worry. 我必須承認那些是很重要的考量，可是它們不適用這個情況，所以無需擔心。

▸ **arise from (= be caused by) 由…引起**

The medical problems I am having now *arised from* some factors the doctor didn't take into account when I was treated for cancer two years ago. 我目前的病況是因兩年前治療癌症時，醫生沒有考慮到某些因素而引起的。

解答 018

解答 **(A) am anxious about 為…焦急不安**

我知道這是為公司好，可是我有點不安，如果瑪麗發現我們密謀讓她被解僱後會如何反應。

選項 (A)am anxious about 為…焦急不安 (B)am ashamed of 以…為恥 (C)am aware of 意識到，知道

補充例句

▸ **be ashamed of 以…為恥**

I know you're just trying to have some harmless fun, but I'*m* really *ashamed of* your behavior right now; it's embarrassing. 我知道你想要開個無傷大雅的玩笑，可是我現在真的以你的行為為恥，真的很不好意思。

▸ **be aware of (= be conscious of, having knowledge or consciousness) 意識到，知道**

I originally thought I was all alone on the street, but I soon *was aware of* someone following me. 我本來以為我是一個人在街上，可是很快地，我發現有人跟著我。

Luisa may seem like a self-centered psycho when you first meet her, but I've found her to be extremely loyal—she'll never ________.

A be on her back

B be at her friends' back

C turn her back on friends

We were all expecting John to kick the bucket within a few weeks, but miraculously his condition took a turn ________ and now he's completely cured.

A for the benefit of

B for the better

C get the better of

解答 019

解答 **(C) turn her back on friends 背叛、拋棄朋友**

初次見路易莎會以為她是個自我中心的瘋子，可是我發現她非常忠實，絕對不會背叛朋友。

選項 (A)be on her back 臥病在床 (B)be at her friends' back 支持朋友 (C)turn her back on friends 背叛、拋棄朋友

補充例句

- **be on one's back (= be ill in bed) 臥病在床**
  Since his unfortunate motorcycle accident, Tim has *been on his back* in the hospital for the last two weeks. 在不幸的摩托車意外之後，提姆過去兩週都躺在醫院的病床上。
- **be at one's back 支持，維護**
  Lenny can afford to take chances on the stock market because he's got rich parents *at his back*—they'll always cover for him. 藍尼可以冒著在股市賠錢的風險，因為他有富有的父母在背後支持，他們永遠會幫他的。

解答 020

解答 **(B) for the better 好轉**

我們都以為約翰在幾週內就會過世，但是奇蹟似地，他的狀況好轉，現在已經完全痊癒了。

選項 (A)for the benefit of 為了…的利益[好處] (B)for the better 好轉 (C)get the better of 打敗，勝過

補充例句

- **for the benefit of 為了…的利益[好處]**
  We're taking donations *for the benefit of* victims of both the Pakistani floods and the Haitian earthquake. 我們在募款，為了幫助巴基斯坦洪水和海地地震的災民。
- **get the better of (= defeat sb) 打敗，勝過**
  The player's temper *got the better of* him and he ended up losing the match to a much inferior player. 這位選手的脾氣控制了他，所以最後輸給了一個差他很多的選手。

Since he got ________ the HSR train about an hour ago, I imagine he'll be arriving here in Taichung any minute now.

A on board

B boast of

C out of breath

I'm pretty sure that Derek had nothing to do with the animal's death—he simply ________ cruelty to animals.

A isn't cautious of

B isn't certain of

C isn't capable of

解答 021

解答 **(A) on board 上船、飛機等交通工具**
既然他一小時前已經搭上高鐵，我猜也應該快到臺中了。

選項 (A)on board 上船、飛機等交通工具 (B)boast of 自誇，誇耀 (C)out of breath 喘不過氣來

補充例句

- **boast of [about] 自誇，誇耀**
This city is so crazy about baseball that it not only *boasts of* one, but two professional baseball teams. 這個城市很瘋棒球，他們自豪於兩隊職業棒球隊。
- **out of breath 喘不過氣來**
You've gone up only one flight of stairs and you're already *out of breath*. What a wimp you are! 你才爬一層樓就喘不過氣來。真是弱掉了！

解答 022

解答 **(C) isn't capable of 能夠，有能力**
我很確定德瑞克跟這隻動物的死亡沒有關係，他沒有對動物殘忍的能力。

選項 (A)isn't cautious of 謹慎於 (B)isn't certain of 有把握，確定 (C)isn't capable of 能夠，有能力

補充例句

- **be cautious of 謹慎於**
It's often wise to proceed slowly and make sure things are done right, but in this case I'd *be cautious of* moving too slow—the market is simply too competitive. 不要躁進而確定事情做對是明智的，但在這件事情上，我太謹慎而動作太慢了，市場實在太競爭了。
- **be certain of (= be sure of) 有把握，確定**
Vivian is a married woman, but I saw her kissing Tony the other day in the custodian's closet—I'*m certain of* it. 薇薇安已經結婚，可是前幾天我看見她在警衛室親吻湯尼，我很確定。

I may not ________ the Christian God, but that doesn't mean I don't recognize the existence of some all-powerful force or being.

A **be on behalf of**

B **believe in**

C **benefit from**

He's so determined to show off his wealth that he'll buy a Rolex, a Rolls Royce or a private yacht ________.

A **in any case**

B **at any price**

C **in the case of**

解答 023

解答 **(B) believe in 相信，信仰**

我也許不相信基督教的神，可是這並不表示我不相信有一些全能力量的存在。

選項 (A)on behalf of 以…名義 (B)believe in 相信，信仰 (C)benefit from 受益，得到好處

補充例句

- **on behalf of (= as the representative of) 以…名義**

  On behalf of the people of this city, we offer you a hearty welcome and the key to the city—enjoy your visit here! 以這城市的人民的名義，我們獻給您誠摯的歡迎和城市鎖鑰，希望您在這裡玩得愉快！

- **benefit from 受益，得到好處**

  In my opinion, kids won't *benefit* at all *from* learning English in primary school—they're better off waiting until they're in their teens. 我的看法是，孩子在小學上英語課是無益的，應該等到青少年時再學。

解答 024

解答 **(B) at any price 不惜任何代價**

他決心要炫耀財富，所以不惜代價要買勞力士、勞斯萊斯或是私人遊艇。

選項 (A)in any case 無論如何 (B)at any price 不惜任何代價 (C)in the case of 至於…，就…而言

補充例句

- **in any case 無論如何**

  In any case, we probably should liquidate our assets before market factors make it unfavorable to do so. 無論如何，我們應在市場狀況對我們不利前先清算我們的資產。

- **in the case of 至於…，就…而言**

  Naomi has been a faithful wife for 20 years—*in the case of* Nancy, however, she's had about as many lovers as there are stars in the sky. 娜歐蜜當了二十年忠實的太太；至於南西，她的情人則多如天上的星星。

Our company's dress code is fairly relaxed compared to other companies, but ________ are jeans, T-shirts and sandals allowed.

A in no case

B center our attention on

C for certain

Jenny is a tulip fan, but unfortunately when she went to the Netherlands the tulips weren't ________ yet—she arrived three weeks too early.

A in brief

B in blossom

C in bulk

解答 025

解答 **(A) in no case 絕不**

我們公司的服裝要求跟其他公司比起來算是輕鬆的，可是絕不允許牛仔褲、T恤和涼鞋。

選項 (A)in no case 絕不 (B)center our attention on 集中我們的注意力在…上 (C)for certain 確定地，有把握地

補充例句

- **center one's attention on (= focus one's attention on)** 把某人的注意力集中在…上
  There were hundreds of beautiful and intelligent girls for Nick to choose from, but for some reason he *centered his attention on* the dumb and ugly one. 有上百位漂亮且聰明的女孩讓尼克選擇，可是不知為何，他選擇了又笨又醜的那一位。
- **for certain (= for sure)** 確定地，有把握地
  Your accusation of Dick embezzling money from the company's coffers is very serious—do you know he's been doing it *for certain*? 你對於狄克占用公司保險箱的公款這個指控很嚴重，你確定他有這麼做嗎？

解答 026

解答 **(B) in blossom 開花**

珍妮是鬱金香迷，可是很遺憾，當她到荷蘭時，鬱金香還沒開，她早到了三週。

選項 (A)in brief 簡言之 (B)in blossom 開花 (C)in bulk 散裝的，成批的

補充例句

- **in brief (= in as few words as possible)** 簡言之
  Put a sock in the long speech, Henry—just tell me what happened at the meeting *in brief*. 長話短說，亨利，簡短地告訴我會議中發生了什麼事。
- **in bulk** 散裝的，成批的
  In the old days I used to buy film *in bulk* to save money, but now memory cards have made film purchasing obsolete. 我以前會為了省錢大量買底片，可是現在記憶卡終結了買底片的時代。

Even though I can't ________ stealing my girlfriend, I'd still like to rip your lungs out nevertheless.

(A) **begin with**

(B) **be at birth**

(C) **blame you for**

You've got to feign ignorance if Lisa ever finds out about this—there's no telling what she'll do if she finds out we had planned this ________ .

(A) **at the back of**

(B) **behind her back**

(C) **is based on [upon]**

解答 027

解答 **(C) blame you for 責怪**

雖然我不能責怪你搶走我的女朋友，但我還是很想把你大卸八塊。

選項 (A)begin with 以…開始 (B)at birth 在出生時 (C)blame you for 責怪

補充例句

▸ **begin with 以…開始**

to begin with (= first of all) 首先，第一（常用於開始語）

You can't understand why you're not popular here? Well *to begin with*, you're lazy, irresponsible and arrogant. 你不知道自己為什麼不受歡迎嗎？首先，你又懶、又不負責任、又自大。

▸ **at birth 在出生時**

He was blind *at birth*, but as a result of medical advances his sight was restored when he was in high school. 他出生時眼睛是看不見的，可是隨著醫學進步，他的視力在高中時恢復了。

解答 028

解答 **(B) behind her back 背著她密謀**

如果莉莎一旦發現，你一定要假裝不知道，你知道她如果發現我們背著她密謀這計畫會怎麼反應。

選項 (A)at the back of 在…後面 (B)behind her back 背著她密謀 (C)is based on [upon] 基於

補充例句

▸ **at the back of (= behind) 在…後面**

There is a cell phone store *at the back of* the hotel, Mr. Johnson—you might be able to get a spare battery there. 飯店後面有一家手機店，強森先生，你應該可以在那裡買到備用電池。

▸ **be based on [upon] 基於**

The movie *is based on* a true story, though the director took liberties with what really happened for dramatic effect. 雖然導演為了戲劇效果自行更改部分事實，但這部電影還是根據一個真實故事拍攝而成。

Because that bag of wind took so long to finish his speech, most of the audience had either left or lost interest by the time I was allowed to ________.

A take the floor

B on business

C at any rate

Even though Mrs. Parker was ________ last week, her condition worsened almost immediately and she was readmitted the following week.

A adjacent to

B put on airs

C discharged from hospital

解答 029

解答 **(A) take the floor 起立發言**

因為那個誇張的人說了太久，到我可以發言時，大部分人要不是走了就是沒興趣了。

選項 (A)take the floor 起立發言 (B)on business 出差 (C)at any rate 無論如何

補充例句

▸ **on business 出差**

Well, technically I'm here *on business*, but that doesn't mean I'm not allowed to have some fun before heading back. 原則上我是來出差的，可是不表示我不可以在回去前玩一下。

▸ **at any rate 無論如何**

It's probably too late to reserve train tickets for the Chinese New Year—but I'm going home to Chiayi *at any rate*. 現在買春節火車票可能已經太遲了，可是無論如何我一定要回嘉義的家。

解答 030

解答 **(C) discharged from hospital 出院**

雖然帕克太太上個禮拜出院，但她的狀況又立刻轉壞，所以這個禮拜又住院了。

選項 (A)adjacent to 與…臨近 (B) put on airs 擺架子 (C)discharged from hospital 出院

補充例句

▸ **adjacent to 與…臨近**

There is a diner *adjacent to* the bus station, so if the bus is late we'll still have time to get some grub. 在巴士站旁邊有一間餐廳，所以如果巴士晚到了，我們還是有點時間去吃東西。

▸ **put on airs 擺架子**

Yvonne is really full of herself—she began to *put on airs* for just acting in a karaoke video. 伊芳真的很自大，只不過在一個卡拉OK伴唱帶演出過，就開始擺架子了。

Children are so innocent and so precious that they should not be used as leverage ________ — it just isn't moral.

Ⓐ **at any cost**

Ⓑ **in case**

Ⓒ **access to**

I've been fiddling with this machine for over two hours and I still can't figure out what this sprocket ________.

Ⓐ **appeals to**

Ⓑ **attaches to**

Ⓒ **attends to**

解答 031

解答 **(A) at any cost 無論如何**

小孩子很天真且寶貝，無論如何，他們都真的不該被利用在談判拉鋸上，這樣太不道德了。

選項 (A)at any cost 無論如何 (B)in case 以防萬一 (C)access to 能接近，進入，了解

補充例句

- **in case (= for fear that) 以防萬一**
  Tiffany carries her video camera with her at all times *in case* an opportunity to film something exciting for YouTube pops up. 蒂芬妮總是帶著她的攝影機，以防萬一有機會拍到有趣的東西可以上傳到YouTube。
- **access to 能接近，進入，了解**
  When I go to Bali I won't have *access to* a cell phone or the internet, so if you need to get hold of me you'll have to leave a message at my hotel. 我去峇里島的時候，沒有辦法連接到手機或網路，所以如果你需要找我，你必須在飯店留話。

解答 032

解答 **(B) attaches to 連結，吸附**

我已經花了兩個小時在這個機器上，但我還是搞不懂這個齒輪該接到哪裡。

選項 (A)appeals to 呼籲 (B)attaches to 連結，吸附 (C)attends to 侍候，照料

補充例句

- **appeal to sb for sth 為某事向某人呼籲[懇求]**
  I cannot underestimate the importance of this project, so I must *appeal to* you *for* understanding and support. 我無法低估這個案子的重要性，所以我必須懇求你們大家的體諒和支持。
- **attend to 侍候，照料**
  I hate to be rude, Steven, but I can't help you right now—I have other affairs to *attend to*. 我不想失禮，史蒂芬，可是我現在無法幫你，我有其他事要照料。

Generally speaking, you'll be allowed to work unsupervised, but if you screw anything up you'll have to ________ me.

A amount to

B undertake responsibility for

C answer to

School cancellations are relatively rare in Taiwan—they only happen ________ really bad typhoons or earthquakes.

A on the average

B on the basis of

C in the event of

解答 033

解答 **(C) answer to 負責**

一般而言，你是可以獨立工作的，可是如果你搞砸什麼事，你要讓我知道。

選項 (A)amount to 總計，等於 (B)undertake responsibility for 承擔責任 (C)answer to 負責

補充例句

▸ **amount to 總計，等於**

Your idea sounds great on the surface, but all it *amounts to* is a cosmetics job; it doesn't address the underlying problems at all. 你的想法表面上聽起來不錯，但它只是個化妝過[潤飾過]的東西，完全沒有碰到實質的問題。

▸ **undertake responsibility for 承擔責任**

Because you've repeatedly failed to improve the situation, I'm now going to have Ron *undertake responsibility for* the project. 因為你一直無法改進狀況，所以我要讓容恩接手，承擔你這個案子。

解答 034

解答 **(C) in the event of 萬一，倘若**

在臺灣很少停課，只有在萬一真的發生很嚴重的颱風或地震時才會停課。

選項 (A)on the average 平均 (B)on the basis of 根據…，在…基礎上 (C)in the event of 萬一，倘若

補充例句

▸ **on the average (= on average, on an average) 平均**

The leading team of the league *on the average* enjoys attendence of over 40,000 spectators per game, whereas the lousy team is lucky to have 5,000 people show up. 聯盟中的領先隊伍每場平均都有超過四萬個觀眾，至於比較差的隊伍，最多有五千個觀眾就不錯了。

▸ **on the basis of 根據…，在…基礎上**

On the basis of the huge amount of customer satisfaction that you have received, Don, we've decided to promote you to full manager starting from next week. 唐，基於你得到很高的客戶滿意度，我們決定下週起升你為全職經理。

________ the financial crisis, there was a high default rate in the nation's banking industry.

A **As a result of**

B **In case of**

C **Act on**

I'm completely confused because what you're telling me now is totally ________ what you told me yesterday.

A **in accord with**

B **out of accord with**

C **on your own account**

解答 035

解答 **(A) As a result of 由於…的結果**

由於財務危機的結果，這個國家的銀行產業有很高的拖款欠債率。

選項 (A)As a result of 由於…的結果 (B)In case of 如果，假設 (C)Act on 奉行，按照…行動

補充例句

▸ **in case of 如果，假設**

The school fair is scheduled for next week, but *in case of* unfavorable weather it will be rescheduled for the following month. 學校園遊會預計在下週舉行，可是如果天氣不好，就會改到下個月。

▸ **act on 奉行，按照…行動**

I think we'd better *act on* this opportunity right now before the competition gets wind of it. 在對手得到消息之前，我想現在我們最好把握這個機會行動。

解答 036

解答 **(B) out of accord with 與…不一致**

我完全困惑了，因為你現在告訴我的跟你昨天說的完全不一致。

選項 (A)in accord with 與…一致 (B)out of accord with 與…不一致 (C)on your own account 為你的自身利益

補充例句

▸ **in accord with 與…一致**

Because his ideas are not *in accord with* the doctrine of our church, he has been asked to stop attending services. 因為他的想法跟我們教會的教義不一致，他已被要求不要再參加禮拜。

▸ **on one's own account 為了某人自身的利益**

Originally I thought Lionel was being generous, but in the end I realized he was just doing it *on his own account*. 原本我以為萊諾很大方，可是後來我才知道他是為了自身利益。

I've always trusted your judgement before, but I just can't ________ you on your choice of Wendy for the position of Account Director.

A agree with

B agree to

C abide by

All the employees tried to appear that they were ______ with the boss, even though deep down they thought he was an old fool who should have retired years ago.

A having knowledge of

B adapting themselves to

C in agreement with

解答 037

解答 **(A) agree with 同意(某人)**

我以前一直很信任你的判斷力，可是我無法同意你選擇溫蒂作為會計長的決定。

選項 (A)agree with 同意(某人) (B)agree to 同意(某事) (C)abide by 遵循

補充例句

- **agree to 同意（某事）**

The Argentinian striker was threatening to quit the team but after lengthy negotiations he *agreed to* a new multi-million-dollar contract. 阿根廷隊的前鋒威脅要離開球隊，可是在長期協商下，他同意了數百萬元的新合約。

- **abide by 遵循**

The rich boy was so spoiled that it was very difficult to get him to *abide by* the school's rules just like everybody else. 這個有錢的男孩被寵壞了，所以要讓他跟其他孩子一樣遵守校規很困難。

解答 038

解答 **(C) in agreement with 同意**

所有的職員都嘗試表現他們是同意老闆的，即使他們內心都認為他是個老笨蛋，幾年前就該退休了。

選項 (A)having knowledge of 了解 (B)adapting themselves to 使自己適應於 (C)in agreement with 同意

補充例句

- **have knowledge of 了解**

When finally confronted wtih irrefutable evidence, Mr. Nixon finally confessed to having *had* prior *knowledge of* the Watergate break-in. 當終於要面對無法反駁的證據時，尼克森總統終於承認他在事前就知道水門事件。

- **adapt oneself to (= adjust oneself to) 使自己適應於**

I was really tempted to leave Spain and head straight home but I decided to stick it out and *adapt myself to* the culture. 我真的想要離開西班牙，然後直接回家，可是我決定撐下來，讓自己適應那裡的文化。

Because you have failed to ________ the particulars of our agreement, we have no choice but to sue you for the break of contract.

A conform to

B comply with

C cling to

The American players are much taller than we are, but we ________ them with our speed and teamwork.

A have an advantage over

B have the advantage of

C take advantage of

解答 039

解答 **(B) comply with 遵守**

因為你未能遵守我們協議中的條款，我沒有選擇，只能控告你違約。

選項 (A)conform to 符合 (B)comply with 遵守 (C)cling to 黏附，堅持，遵循

補充例句

▸ **conform to 符合**

I wasn't used to Chinese corporate culture and wanted to rebel at first, but in the end I found it was easier for everybody if I just *conformed to* the way things are done here. 我並不習慣中國的企業文化，一開始也想反抗，可是最後我發現，如果我去配合對大家都比較容易。

▸ **cling to 黏附，堅持，遵循**

He looked like an ignorant old fool at first, but his insisting on *clinging to* the old way of doing things actually earned him praise in the end. 他一開始看起來像個不起眼的老笨蛋，可是他堅持要走老路的結果反而得到讚賞。

解答 040

解答 **(A) have an advantage over 勝過**

美國隊比我們高很多，可是我們勝過他們的是我們的速度和團隊合作。

選項 (A)have an advantage over 勝過 (B)have the advantage of 由於…處於有利條件 (C)take advantage of 利用

補充例句

▸ **have the advantage of 由於…處於有利條件**

I know he has an Ivy League education, but we *have the advantage of* connections and experience in the industry, so don't worry. 我知道他有美國長春藤名校的學歷背景，可是我們的有利條件是我們在業界的關係和經驗，所以別擔心。

▸ **take advantage of 利用**

I was originally going to stay home and clean house today, but I decided to *take advantage of* the great weather to go hiking instead. 我本來要待在家裡整理房子，可是我決定要利用好天氣去爬爬山。

Taipei has improved a lot in recent years I must admit, but I'm used to living in the east and am ________ interested in moving back there.

A above all

B after all

C not at all

It sounded like the idea was going to be implemented within a day or so, but it's already been a month and it's still ________.

A in accordance with

B in addition to

C in the air

解答 041

解答 **(C) not at all 一點也不**

我必須承認，這幾年來臺北進步了很多，可是我已經習慣住在東部，所以一點也沒有興趣要搬回去。

選項 (A) above all 尤其是，最重要的 (B) after all 畢竟，到底 (C) not at all 一點也不

補充例句

▸ **above all 尤其是，最重要的**

An employee must of course be hard-working, honest and punctual, but *above all* he should be as loyal to the company as a dog would be to its master. 身為職員，努力、誠實和準時是當然的，可是最重要的是，對公司的忠誠要像狗之於主人一樣。

▸ **after all 畢竟，到底**

Opera is a distinguished art form for sure, but I am *after all* from Tennessee and I'll take a Willie Nelson tune over Verdi anyway. 歌劇的確是與眾不同的藝術，可是我畢竟是從田納西來的，所以當然比較喜歡威利尼爾森比威爾第多囉！

解答 042

解答 **(C) in the air 不確定**

當時聽起來這個想法在一、兩天內就會實行，但現在都已經一個月了，卻仍舊沒定下來。

選項 (A) in accordance with 依照，根據 (B) in addition to 除…之外 (C) in the air 不確定

補充例句

▸ **in accordance with (= in agreement with) 依照，根據**

Barring special circumstances, students may only drop or add classes *in accordance with* university policy. 除了特殊狀況，學生可能只可以依照學校規定加、退選課。

▸ **in addition to 除…之外**

In addition to sports such as badminton and tennis, I also enjoy reading, learning foreign languages, and investing in the stock market. 除了羽毛球和網球這些運動外，我也喜歡看書、學外語，還有投資股票。

I've put up with this problem for many years, but my patience has finally run out and I want to resolve this problem ________.

A all at once

B once and for all

C all in all

The Chief Editor appreciated my hard work, but warned me not to finish the work ________ for fear the boss would start piling on more and more work later.

A ahead of time

B all in

C allow for

解答 043

解答 **(B) once and for all 一次**

我忍受這個問題很多年了，可是我的耐心終於用完了，而且我決定要把問題一次徹底解決。

選項 (A)all at once 突然 (B)once and for all 一次 (C)all in all 大體上而言

補充例句

▸ **all at once (= suddenly) 突然**

We were just sitting down to dinner when *all at once* the floor started shaking and we all scrambled to get the heck out of the building. 我們正坐著吃晚餐，忽然地板開始搖晃，我們全都逃離這棟樓。

▸ **all in all 大體上而言**

Even though it had its flaws, the concert *all in all* was very entertaining and well worth the price of admission. 雖然有缺點，可是這個音樂會大體而言是很有娛樂性的，而且蠻值回票價的。

解答 044

解答 **(A) ahead of time 提早，提前**

總編很欣賞我的努力工作，可是警告我不要提前把工作做完，不然老闆會開始把更多工作交給我。

選項 (A)ahead of time 提早，提前 (B)all in 累極了 (C)allow for 考慮到

補充例句

▸ **all in 累極了**

Gee, Tom, you look *all in*! You'd better come in, sit down, and relax for a while. 啊，湯姆，你看來累極了！你最好進來，坐下，休息一會兒。

▸ **allow for 考慮到**

When I travel, I like to be flexible and *allow for* changes in my itinerary; so of course I don't like to travel with a group. 當我旅遊時，我喜歡彈性點，而且可以改變行程，所以想當然爾，我不喜歡參加旅行團。

Cathleen ________ her many years of depression ________ her parents' constant pressure to be successful when she was a kid.

A attributes...to

B beats...at

C and...leaves room for

Despite the generous compensation offered, only ________ were willing to work on Christmas day.

A make an attempt to

B make a rule of

C a handful of people

解答 045

解答 **(A) attributes...to 歸因於**

凱瑟琳把她多年來的沮喪情緒歸咎於她父母在她孩提時常給她要成功的壓力。

選項 (A)attributes...to 歸因於 (B)beats...at 在…上打贏… (C)leaves room for... 留有…的餘地

補充例句

▸ **beat...at... 在…上打贏…**

No matter how much you practice, Howard, I don't think you'll ever be able to *beat* Jared *at* tennis—he just has a natural talent for it. 不管你怎麼練習，霍華，我不認為你可以在網球上打敗傑瑞德，他在網球上有天分。

▸ **leave room for... 留有…的餘地**

I'm flattered that you find my Hungarian goulash so delicious, but don't forget to *leave room for* dessert! 你認為我的匈牙利燉牛肉很好吃，讓我受寵若驚，可是請留點肚子吃甜點哦！

解答 046

解答 **(C) a handful of people 少數人**

儘管提供了豐厚的加班津貼，只有少數人願意在聖誕節當天工作。

選項 (A)make an attempt to 試圖做… (B)make a rule of 形成…習慣 (C)a handful of people 少數人

補充例句

▸ **make an attempt at doing sth [to do sth] 試圖做…**

Her friends have encouraged her to *make an attempt at* running for student council because she's so friendly, intelligent, and popular. 她的朋友們鼓勵她嘗試競選學生幹事，因為她很友善、聰明，而且受歡迎。

▸ **make a rule of (doing sth) 形成…習慣**

Because ill health is so prevalent in my family I've *made a rule of* exercising every day and getting plenty of fresh air and sunlight. 因為我家的人身體都不好，所以我養成每天運動的習慣，而且吸收許多的新鮮空氣和陽光。

Sam ________ all the long-distance phone calls related to his business.

(A) **keeps track of**

(B) **has been up to**

(C) **finds fault with**

He spoke English so well that I ________ he was an American.

(A) **took it for granted**

(B) **called for**

(C) **crossed out**

解答 047

解答 **(A) keeps track of 記錄**

山姆記錄與他業務有關的長途電話。

選項 (A) keeps track of 記錄 (B) has been up to 一直忙於… (C) finds fault with 找錯誤

補充例句

- **has been up to 一直忙於**

I haven't seen Jesse for a while. I wonder what he *has been up to.* 我有一陣子沒看到傑西了。不知道他最近在做些什麼。

- **find fault with 找錯誤**

It's quite easy for people to *find fault with* the work of others. 對人們而言，要找出別人工作上的錯誤很容易。

解答 048

解答 **(A) took it for granted 認為理所當然**

他英文說得好極了，我想當然爾以為他是美國人。

選項 (A)took it for granted 認為理所當然 (B)called for 需要 (C)crossed out 劃掉

補充例句

- **call for 需要**

This cake recipe *calls for* some baking soda and we happen to have some here. 這個蛋糕的食譜需要烘焙粉，我們這裡剛好有。

- **cross out 劃掉**

The teacher *crossed out* several incorrect words in my composition. 老師在我的作文裡把一些錯誤的字劃掉。

No matter how hard we tried, we still failed; and it's time for us to ________ and throw in the towel.

A **turn out**

B **break down**

C **give in**

It's the ________, John. I'll never lend you any money any more.

A **once in a blue moon**

B **last straw**

C **by all means**

解答 049

解答 **(C) give in 投降**

不管我們嘗試得多辛苦，還是失敗了，該是我們投降認輸的時候了。

選項 (A)turn out 變成 (B)break down 故障 (C)give in 投降

補充例句

- **turn out 變成**

Most parents wonder how their children will *turn out* as adults. 大部分的父母都會想像他們的孩子長大後會是什麼樣子。

- **break down 故障**

The elevator *broke down*, so we walked all the way up to the top floor. 電梯壞了，所以我們一路爬樓梯上頂樓。

解答 050

解答 **(B) last straw 最後一次**

這是最後一次了，約翰，我再也不會借錢給你。

選項 (A)once in a blue moon 偶爾 (B)last straw 最後一次(C)by all means 當然

補充例句

- **once in a blue moon 偶爾**

Once in a blue moon my family and I eat out at an expensive restaurant. 我們全家偶爾會去昂貴的餐廳吃飯。

- **by all means (= of course) 當然**

If you invite us to the party, then *by all means* we have to return the invitation. 如果你邀請我們去派對，我們當然要回請囉。

It's amazing that Alison has ________ so quickly after a series of personal difficulties.

A landed on her feet

B had under her belt

C put her foot in

I expect to learn a lot, but the professor ______ too little ________ in the lecture.

A threw...a curve

B made...waves

C covered...ground

解答 051

解答 **(A) landed on her feet 重新開始振作**
愛莉森在經歷一連串個人困境後可以很快地再站起來，真的令人激賞。

選項 (A)landed on her feet 重新開始振作 (B)had under her belt 有經驗 (C)put her foot in 自找麻煩

補充例句

▸ **have under one's belt 有經驗**
When Mr. Johnson retired, he *has* 50 years of teaching *under his belt*. 當強森先生退休時，他已經有五十年教學經驗了。

▸ **put one's foot in 自找麻煩**
I really *put my foot in* when I forgot my husband's birthday and didn't buy him anything. 當我忘記我先生的生日，也沒有買東西給他時，我就給自己找了麻煩了。

解答 052

解答 **(C) covered...ground 涉及**
我期待學到很多，可是教授在講課中涉及的範圍很少。

選項 (A)threw...a curve 製造臨時問題 (B)made...waves 引起紛亂 (C)covered...ground 涉及

補充例句

▸ **throw (someone) a curve 製造臨時問題**
The supervisor asked us to stick to the agenda and not to *throw her any curves*. 主任要求我們要緊跟著計畫，不要臨時出狀況。

▸ **make waves 引起紛亂**
The director doesn't appreciate any employee who tends to *make waves*. 主管不喜歡任何會製造紛亂的職員。

Don't expect me to agree with you. It's absolutely ________.

A **out of the question**

B **face-to-face**

C **on the ball**

Once a child becomes accustomed to eating snacks, it's difficult to ________.

A **kick around**

B **kick the habit**

C **kick the bucket**

解答 053

解答 **(A) out of the question 不可能**

不要期待我會同意你。這是絕對不可能的。

選項 (A)out of the question 不可能 (B)face-to-face 面對面 (C)on the ball 機靈的

補充例句

▸ **face-to-face 面對面**

The teacher asks to talk with me *face-to-face* about my son's troubles. 老師要求跟我面對面談一下我兒子的問題。

▸ **on the ball 機靈的**

Emily was certainly *on the ball* when she remembered to confirm the reservation. None of the rest of us remembered. 愛蜜莉真是很機靈，記得去確認訂房。我們其餘的人沒一個記得。

解答 054

解答 **(B) kick the habit 戒掉習慣**

一旦孩子習慣吃零食，就很難戒掉。

選項 (A)kick around 一起討論 (B)kick the habit 戒掉習慣 (C)kick the bucket 去世

補充例句

▸ **kick around 一起討論**

My friends didn't accept my suggestion in the beginning, but later they were finally willing to *kick* it *around* for a while. 我的朋友一開始不接受我的建議，可是後來他們終於願意討論一下。

▸ **kick the bucket 去世**

If Tom had had that surgery in time, he wouldn't have *kicked the bucket*. 如果湯姆當初有即時做手術，他就不會過世了。

I know why you don't want to cook Thanksgiving dinner this year. I think you're ______.

A dragging your feet

B wasting your breath

C losing your touch

I was ______ all day yesterday about the presentation I had to give to the board.

A on the whole

B on edge

C touch and go

解答 055

解答 **(C) losing your touch 手藝不如前**

我知道你今年不想煮感恩節大餐的原因。我猜你手藝不如前了。

選項 (A)dragging your feet 卻步，退縮 (B)wasting your breath 浪費力氣 (C)losing your touch 手藝不如前

補充例句

- **drag one's feet 卻步，退縮**
  Mia seemed willing to host the dinner party, but now she's *dragging her feet*. 米雅本來願意主辦這個晚餐派對，可是現在她退縮了。
- **waste one's breath 浪費力氣**
  You're *weasting your breath* arguing with Stanley any longer. He will never change. 你跟史丹利爭論是浪費力氣。他永遠不會改變的。

解答 056

解答 **(B) on edge 緊張**

我昨天一整天都因為要跟董事會做的一個簡報而緊張。

選項 (A)on the whole 整體而言 (B)on edge 緊張 (C)touch and go 很難說，不確定

補充例句

- **on the whole 整體來說**
  On the whole, this year has been a good year for all of us. 整體來說，今年對我們大家而言是很好的一年。
- **touch and go 不確定**
  The outcome of the soccer final was *touch and go* for the entire match. 這個足球決賽的結果在整場球賽進行中一直不確定。

After war began, the two countries ______ diplomatic relations.

A **laid off**

B **wore off**

C **broke off**

The heavy rains we have recently ______ serious flooding.

A **bring about**

B **bring out**

C **bring back**

解答 057

解答 **(C) broke off 絕交，終止**

戰爭開始後，這兩個國家的外交關係就終止了。

選項 (A)laid off 放棄，遠離 (B)wore off 逐漸消失 (C)broke off 絕交，終止

補充例句

▸ **lay off 放棄，遠離**

If you want to lose weight, you have to *lay off* sweet things. 如果你想減肥，一定要放棄甜食。

▸ **wear off 逐漸消失**

My stomachache isn't serious and it normally *wears off* after a few minutes. 我胃痛不太嚴重，而且通常幾分鐘就好了。

解答 058

解答 **(A) bring about 帶來**

最近的大雨帶來嚴重的淹水。

選項 (A)bring about 帶來 (B)bring out 拿出來 (C)bring back 送還

補充例句

▸ **bring out 拿出來**

My mother *brought out* some snacks for my friends and me. 我母親端出一些點心給我和我的朋友吃。

▸ **bring back 送還**

Could you *bring back* the dress you borrowed from me? I need it for a party. 你可以把上次跟我借的衣服還回來嗎？我需要穿它去參加派對。

When the campfire ________, we saw the embers glowing in the dark.

A ripped off

B died down

C died out

If I were ________, I wouldn't take too many classes this semester.

A drawing the line at

B keeping my word

C in your shoes

解答 059

解答 **(B) died down 熄滅**

當營火熄滅時，我們看見黑暗中的餘燼閃亮。

選項 (A)ripped off 剝削 (B)died down 熄滅 (C)died out 滅絕，絕種

補充例句

- **rip off 剝削**

The car dealership certainly *ripped* me *off* when I bought this car. It has broken down a lot since I bought it. 我買車時，那個車商一定坑了我很多錢。從購買到現在它壞了很多次。

- **die out 滅絕，絕種**

Scientists are still trying to find out exactly why dinosaurs *died out*. 科學家仍在嘗試找出恐龍會滅絕的原因。

解答 060

解答 **(C) in your shoes 站在你的立場**

如果我是你，我這學期不會選太多課。

選項 (A)drawing the line at 絕對不容許 (B)keeping my word 信守承諾 (C)in your shoes 站在你的立場

補充例句

- **draw the line at (= refuse to consider) 絕對不容許**

I don't mind helping you out sometimes, but I *draw the line at* lending you money. 我不介意偶爾幫助你一下，可是絕對不借你錢。

- **keep one's word 信守承諾**

Susan always intends to *keep her word*, but invariably the end result is that she breaks her word. 蘇珊總是嘗試要信守承諾，可是最後總是打破承諾。

When an employee ________ in work, he will be fired by the supervisor.

A **plays by ear**

B **gets out of line**

C **looks into**

I always have to ________ my childen about cleaning up the house and doing chores.

A **keep after**

B **fix up**

C **be had**

解答 061

解答 **(B) gets out of line 違反規定**

當一位職員在工作上違反規定時，會被主管解僱。

選項 (A)plays by ear 隨性行事 (B)gets out of line 違反規定 (C) looks into 調查

補充例句

- **play by ear 隨性行事**

Whenever I'm planning a trip, I tend to *play* it *by ear* because I think it's more fun. 每當我計畫旅遊時，我試著隨性點，因為我覺得這樣比較好玩。

- **look into 調查**

There was an accident down the street last night and the Police is now *looking into* this matter. 昨天晚上在這條街上發生了意外，警察正在調查這個案子。

解答 062

解答 **(A) keep after 提醒**

我總是需要提醒我的小孩，保持家裡整潔和做家事。

選項 (A)keep after 提醒 (B)fix up 修理 (C)be had 被騙

補充例句

- **fix up 修理**

Instead of buying an expensive new dog house, we bought an older one and *fixed* it *up*. 我們沒有買昂貴的新狗屋，我們買了個舊的，並且修理一下。

- **be had 被騙**

Judy told me that she had *been had* for buying a fake watch at a souvenior store. 茱蒂告訴我她在一間紀念品店被騙了，買了一隻假手錶。

Would you ________ moving that sofa over here?

Ⓐ give me a big hand

Ⓑ get through to

Ⓒ give me a hand

I'll have to ________ in the office for a while until I get the chance to talk with my boss.

Ⓐ hang around

Ⓑ let slide

Ⓒ rub it in

解答 063

解答 **(C) give me a hand 幫助我**

你可以幫我把那張沙發搬來這裡嗎？

選項 (A)give me a big hand 為我鼓掌、拍手 (B)get through to 溝通 (C)give me a hand 幫助我

補充例句

▸ **give...a big hand 為…鼓掌、拍手**

After that young student finished telling her story, people *gave* her *a big hand*. 在那個年輕學生說完故事後，大家為她熱烈地鼓掌。

▸ **get through to 溝通**

When traveling to France, it is difficult to *get through to* people there because they don't speak English. 到法國旅行時，很難跟當地人溝通，因為他們不說英文。

解答 064

解答 **(A) hang around 停留在某處**

我必須要待在辦公室一會兒，等到我有機會跟老闆說話。

選項 (A)hang around 停留在某處 (B)let slide 忽略(某事) (C) rub it in 取笑某人

補充例句

▸ **let slide 忽略(某事)**

I should have paid my bill instead of *letting* it *slide*. Now my phone is out of service. 我應該付我的帳單而不要忽略它。現在我的電話不通了。

▸ **rub it in 取笑某人**

Sue finally beat John at porkers and she's been *rubbing it in* about that. 蘇終於在撲克牌上打贏了約翰，而她就一直取笑他。

We've been ________ my son's lies too many times to be deceived once again.

A covered for

B traded in

C fallen for

Paula decided to ________ her sister after their arguments about arrangements for house chores.

A make up with

B make up

C look up

解答 065

解答 **(C) fallen for 相信**

我們相信我兒子的謊言太多次了，所以不願意再次被他欺騙。

選項 (A)covered for 代班，掩護 (B)traded in 折舊交換 (C)fallen for 相信

補充例句

▸ **cover for 代班，掩護**

I have an important audition this afternoon. Could you *cover for* me? 我今天下午有一個很重要的試鏡。你可以幫我代班嗎？

▸ **trade in 折舊交換**

The dealer asked me if I want to *trade in* my old car for a new model. 經銷商問我想不想用我的舊車折換一部新車。

解答 066

解答 **(A) make up with 和好**

寶拉和她姊姊為了家事吵了一架後，決定和好。

選項 (A)make up with 和好 (B)make up 補考，補課 (C)look up 看好

補充例句

▸ **make up 補考，補課**

Juliana took a sick leave from school, so she has to *make up* the exams today. 茱莉安娜之前跟學校請病假，所以她今天要補考。

▸ **look up 看好**

The president is elated to announce that things are *looking up* for the company in the first quarter. 總裁很高興地宣布公司第一季的狀況看好。

The plumber didn't fix the toilet, instead, he ________ even more.

A messed it up

B cut it short

C screwed it up

After 40 years of service to this company, the president will ________ next month.

A step in

B step down

C step on it

解答 067

解答 **(C) screwed it up 弄壞**

水電工沒有把馬桶修好，反而使它壞得更嚴重。

選項 (A)messed it up 弄錯 (B)cut it short 把…縮短 (C)screwed it up 弄壞

補充例句

▸ **mess up 弄錯**

Jason really *messed up* on the final exam and he's very upset about it. 傑森期末考真的考砸了，他因此很不開心。

▸ **cut short 把…縮短**

We had to *cut* our trip *short* because of the coming thunder storm. 我們必須要把旅程縮短，因為暴風雨即將來臨。

解答 068

解答 **(B) step down 卸下職務**

在公司服務四十年後，總裁在下個月即將卸下職務。

選項 (A)step in 介入，涉入 (B)step down 卸下職務 (C)step on it 開始工作

補充例句

▸ **step in 介入，涉入**

This is my own business, I'll appreciate if you don't *step in* too much. 這是我自己的事，如果你不要介入太多，我會很感謝你。

▸ **step on it 開始工作**

We've got only two hours to get ready with the presentation, we really need to *step on it* right away. 我們只有兩個小時的時間把簡報做好，我們真的要馬上開始工作了。

The teacher agreed to ________ the deadline of submitting the papers until next Monday.

A **hold out**

B **hold over**

C **hold off**

The company didn't ________ to the staff's demands to shorten their working hours. Instead, they fired them.

A **give out**

B **give in**

C **give off**

解答 069

解答 **(C) hold off 延期**

老師同意將交報告的截止日期延後到下週一。

選項 (A)hold out 足夠 (B)hold over 延續 (C)hold off 延期

補充例句

- **hold out 足夠**

The supply of food and water didn't *hold out*, so we had to cut short our camping trip. 我們在食物和水的補充上不夠，所以必須把露營旅程縮短。

- **hold over 延續**

The board has decided to *hold* discussion of this issue *over* until next meeting. 董事會決定要將這個議題的討論延續到下次的會議。

解答 070

解答 **(B) give in 投降，妥協**

公司沒有妥協接受員工的要求而縮短工作時數，反而是解僱了他們。

選項 (A)give out 用光 (B)give in 投降，妥協 (C)give off 散發…香味

補充例句

- **give out 用光**

I had to shorten my trip in Europe because my money *gave out*. 我想要縮短我在歐洲的旅程，因為我的錢用光了。

- **give off 散發…香味**

Did you smell the scent that the flowers *gave off*? 你有聞到那些花散發的香味嗎？

We need to attract more investors as soon as possible, or the company may ________.

- A go to the wall
- B weather the storm
- C draw a veil over

She had a great plan to start her own business but it's ________ . She's now a content mother with 2 kids.

- A in blissful ignorance
- B safe and sound
- C dead in the water

解答 071

解答 **(A) go to the wall 破產**
我們必須盡快吸引更多投資者，不然公司可能會破產。

選項 (A)go to the wall 破產 (B)weather the storm 突破困境 (C)draw a veil over 避而不談，不願觸及

補充例句

▸ **weather the storm 突破困境**
The company underwent a lot of problems last year, but it *weathered the storm* and now it's doing pretty well. 公司去年經歷了許多問題，不過還是突破困境，而且現在營運得不錯。

▸ **draw a veil over 避而不談，不願觸及**
Dan's willing to talk about anything, but he prefers to *draw a veil over* his unhappy childhood. 丹願意談論任何事，可是他不願提及不愉快的童年。

解答 072

解答 **(C) dead in the water 沒有下文，無疾而終**
她曾經有個發展自己事業的偉大計畫，可是後來無疾而終。她現在是擁有兩個孩子的知足母親。

選項 (A)in blissful ignorance 寧可不知道 (B)safe and sound 安全且狀況良好 (C)dead in the water 沒有下文，無疾而終

補充例句

▸ **in blissful ignorance 寧可不知道**
I know there might be problems, but I don't want to know, instead, I'd like to remain *in blissful ignorance*. 我知道可能有問題，可是我不想知道，我反而寧可不知道。

▸ **safe and sound 安全且狀況良好**
I am not sure whether those china will arrive *safe and sound* by post. 我不確定那些瓷器是否可以安全且狀況良好地透過郵寄抵達。

We're ________ because my daughter is still waiting for the results of her entrance exam.

A putting our holiday plans on the back burner

B throwing in the towel

C standing a chance

All the food and water in the supermarkets were ________ by residents before the typhoon came.

A bought out

B bought up

C cleared up

解答 073

解答 **(A) putting our holiday plans on the back burner** 將假期計畫擱置

我們把假期計畫擱置，因為我的女兒還在等她入學考試的結果。

選項 (A)putting our holiday plans on the back burner 將假期計畫擱置 (B)throwing in the towel 放棄 (C)standing a chance 有機會

補充例句

- **throw in the towel** 放棄

  As I found that I couldn't persuade her, I think I'll *throw in the towel* and just let her do what she wants to. 我發現我無法說服她，我想放棄了，就隨她任意去做。

- **stand a chance** 有機會

  Our school baseball team *stands a* good *chance* of winning the university league this year. 我們學校的棒球隊有大好良機可以贏得今年的大學聯賽。

解答 074

解答 **(B) bought up** 買光貨品

在颱風來臨前，超市裡所有的食物和水都被附近居民買光了。

選項 (A)bought out 收購企業 (B)bought up 買光貨品 (C)cleared up 讓人清楚了解

補充例句

- **buy out** 收購企業

  For different reasons, big companies often *buy out* smaller companies which are having financial difficulties. 由於各種原因，大公司通常會收購面臨財務困境的小公司。

- **clear up** 讓人清楚了解

  The teacher spent two hours trying to *clear up* the students' confusion about some certain English grammar points. 老師花了兩個小時試著讓學生了解他們在英文文法上的一些困惑。

Sometimes it's hard to know what he really means, because he ________ too much.

- A beats around the bush
- B fools around
- C loses his head

We all tried to warn him about the risk he's taking, but he ________ whatever we said.

- A diced with death
- B raced against time
- C turned a deaf ear to

解答 075

解答 **(A) beats around the bush 拐彎抹角**

有時候不太容易知道他要說什麼，因為他非常地不直接。

選項 (A)beats around the bush 拐彎抹角 (B)fools around 閒晃，虛度光陰 (C)loses his head 慌張失措

補充例句

- **fool around** 閒晃，虛度光陰

I wish my son would stop *fooling around* and start to do something more meaningful. 我希望我兒子不要再閒晃，而應該開始做一些比較有意義的事了。

- **lose one's head** 慌張失措

If you hadn't *lost your head*, you wouldn't have made that huge mistake. 如果你沒有慌張失措，你就不會犯下這麼大的錯誤。

解答 076

解答 **(C) turned a deaf ear to 聽不進去**

我們都試著警告他風險，可是他完全聽不進去。

選項 (A)diced with death 玩命，冒生命危險 (B)raced against time 跟時間賽跑 (C)turned a deaf ear to 聽不進去

補充例句

- **dice with death** 玩命，冒生命危險

Driving a 20-year-old car is like *dicing with death* because you never know when it will break down. 開這部二十年的老車好像在玩命，因為你不知道它什麼時候會壞掉。

- **race against time** 跟時間賽跑

The patient was very ill and it was a *race against time* to find her an organ doner. 這位病患病得很嚴重，幫她找器官捐贈者是件跟時間賽跑的事。

Jim was caught cheating during the exam and is now going to ________.

A find his feet

B face the music

C speak too soon

What is ________ of the preparation of the annual board meeting? Is everything on schedule?

A the state of play

B the fact of the matter

C the survival of the fittest

解答 077

解答 **(B) face the music 面對現實，接受處罰**
吉姆在考試中作弊，現在要接受處罰。

選項 (A)find his feet 進入狀況 (B)face the music 面對現實，接受處罰 (C)speak too soon 說得太早

補充例句

▸ **find one's feet 進入狀況**
The new students are still *finding their feet* here; let's us give them more time. 這些學生還在進入狀況，我們給他們一些時間吧！

▸ **speak too soon 說得太早**
Look at the clouds. I *spoke too soon* when I said it's going to be clear today. 你看那烏雲。我說今天會放晴真是說得太早了。

解答 078

解答 **(A) the state of paly 狀況**
理事年會準備的狀況如何？所有事都照行程走嗎？

選項 (A)the state of play 狀況 (B)the fact of the matter 事實是 (C) the survival of the fittest 適者生存

補充例句

▸ **the fact of the matter 事實是**
I can't meet you tonight. *The fact of the matter* is that I have to work overtime. 我今晚無法見你。事實是我必須要加班。

▸ **the survival of the fittest 適者生存**
It's tough if you want to become successful in show biz; it is a question of *the survival of the fittest*. 要在娛樂事業上成功是很困難的，這是適者生存的問題。

The referee ________ the game because of the heavy rain.

A put off

B called off

C put out

Where did you ________ that brilliant idea? I really like it and I'm sure it will work.

A brush up on

B come up with

C figure out

解答 079

解答 **(B) called off 取消**

因為大雨，裁判決定取消比賽。

選項 (A)put off 拖延 (B)called off 取消 (C)put out 滅火

補充例句

- **put off 拖延**
  The teacher always reminds us not to *put off* things until the last minute. 老師總是提醒我們不要把事情拖到最後一分鐘。
- **put out 滅火**
  Sorry I didn't see the "Non-smoking" sign here. I'll *put out* my cigarette right away. 抱歉，我沒有看到『禁煙』的標誌。我現在馬上把煙熄掉。

解答 080

解答 **(B) come up with 發現，想到**

你怎麼想到這麼棒的主意的？我真的很喜歡它，而且我確定它一定可行。

選項 (A)brush up on 重新溫習 (B)come up with 發現，想到 (C)figure out 理解，弄懂

補充例句

- **brush up on 重新溫習**
  You'd better *brush up on* your English before you study abroad this coming September. 你最好在九月出國唸書前把英文溫習一下。
- **figure out 理解，弄懂**
  I've finally *figured out* the problem with my computer and fixed it. 我終於弄懂了我電腦的問題，而且修理好了。

We were just talking with each other, and ________, Mary shouted out loud because she saw an accident.

A all along

B ahead of time

C all of a sudden

We thought the boss would talk to us for hours, but he finished talking ________ and asked us to go back to work.

A in no time

B for good

C by heart

解答 081

解答 **(C) all of a sudden 忽然間**

我們正在說話，忽然間瑪麗大叫一聲，因為她看見了一個意外。

選項 (A)all along 一直 (B)ahead of time 事前 (C)all of a sudden 忽然間

補充例句

▸ **all along 一直**

Did you know *all along* that you didn't need to go to school today? Or you had no idea about it? 你一直都知道今天不需要上學嗎？還是你並不知情？

▸ **ahead of time 事前**

If I knew *ahead of time* that you were coming, I would cook extra dishes. 如果我事前知道你會來，我會多煮一些菜。

解答 082

解答 **(A) in no time 很快**

我們以為老闆會跟我們說上幾個小時，可是他很快地說完了，就叫我們回座位工作。

選項 (A)in no time 很快 (B)for good 永遠 (C)by heart 用記憶的

補充例句

▸ **for good 永遠**

Chuck's contract here is over and he's going back to the States *for good*. Too bad we won't be able to see him a lot. 恰克在這裡的合約到期了，他要永遠回美國了。可惜我們無法常看到他了。

▸ **by heart 用記憶的**

Cynthia works so hard that she knows a lot of good English speeches *by heart*. 辛西亞很努力，所以她能夠背誦很多有名的英語演講。

Even though you have a hard time with math, you shouldn't ________ and quit school.

A take hold of

B get carried away

C keep away from

Do you happen to have the ________ catalog of that store? I want to see if they have any chairs on sale.

A up to date

B out of date

C first-rate

解答 083

解答 **(B) get carried away 離開**

雖然你的數學學得很痛苦，也不需要離校、休學啊！

選項 (A)take hold of 握著 (B)get carried away 離開 (C)keep away from 避開

補充例句

- **take hold of 握著**

The sweet young boy is *taking hold of* his grandpa's arm and leading him across the street. 這個可愛的小男孩握著他祖父的手帶他過馬路。

- **keep away from 避開**

Please make sure to *keep* the children *away from* danger. As their teacher, we're responsible for their safety. 請確定讓孩子遠離危險。身為他們的老師，我們要為他們的安全負責。

解答 084

解答 **(A) up to date 最新的**

你不會剛好有那間店最新的目錄吧？我想要看看他們有沒有椅子在特賣。

選項 (A)up to date 最新的 (B)out of date 過時的 (C)first-rate 最佳的，一流的

補充例句

- **out of date 過時的**

Come on! Your idea is really *out of date*. I suggest that you get out of the house and explore the world. 拜託！你的主意真是過時。我建議你多出門體驗世界。

- **first-rate 最佳的，一流的**

His work is known as the *first-rate* among all young designers. He will soon have his own brand name and start his own business. 他的作品在所有年輕設計師中被公認是一流的。他很快會有自己的品牌，開始自己的事業。

There's no point asking me to lend you a hand. I'm actually ________.

A second to none

B pie in the sky

C in the same boat

Since you made the mistake, you shouldn't have had somebody else to ________ for you. You should face the music.

A make no mistake

B jump the gun

C carry the can

解答 085

解答 **(C) in the same boat 處境相同**

叫我幫你忙是沒有意義的。我其實跟你狀況一樣。

選項 (A)second to none 第一名 (B)pie in the sky 遙不可及 (C)in the same boat 處境相同

補充例句

- **second to none** 第一名

When it comes to cooking, my mother is *second to none*. She can fix a table for 10 with ease. 說到廚藝，我母親是最厲害的。她可以輕易地辦一桌十個人的筵席。

- **pie in the sky** 遙不可及

All his promises were *pie in the sky*; he fullfilled none of them. 他的承諾都是遙不可及的，沒有一個實現。

解答 086

解答 **(C) carry the can 背黑鍋**

既然是你犯了錯，就不應該讓別人幫你背黑鍋。你應該自己去面對懲罰。

選項 (A)make no mistake 毫無疑問地 (B)jump the gun 太性急 (C)carry the can 背黑鍋

補充例句

- **make no mistake** 毫無疑問地

You just go ahead and quit, but *make no mistake*, you will regret some day. 你就辭職吧，不過毫無疑問地，你有一天會後悔的。

- **jump the gun** 太性急

He has *jumped the gun* by making a flight reservation; he's not even sure whether he'll be able to leave from work. 他很性急地訂了飛機機位，他甚至都不確定是否可以向公司請假。

Sammi has a headache and she feels a bit ________ .

A under the weather

B under the cosh

C gloom and gloom

I can't talk with Mike. We don't really ________ about most things.

A pick and choose

B come rain or shine

C see eye to eye

解答 087

解答 **(A) under the weather 不舒服**

珊美頭痛，而且她感覺不舒服。

選項 (A)under the weather 不舒服 (B)under the cosh 在壓力下 (C)gloom and gloom 憂鬱，悲觀

補充例句

- **under the cosh 在壓力下**

  As final exams are on the way, Craig is *under the cosh* preparing for that. 期末考要到了，克雷格很有壓力地在準備考試。

- **gloom and gloom 憂鬱，悲觀**

  It was *gloom and gloom* for Luke last year. Not only did he have problems at work, but also his wife left him. 去年路克很憂鬱。不僅工作上有問題，而且他太太離開了他。

解答 088

解答 **(C) see eye to eye 意見一致**

我無法跟麥克說話。我們在大部分事情上都意見不合。

選項 (A)pick and choose 仔細慎選 (B)come rain or shine 無論如何 (C)see eye to eye 意見一致

補充例句

- **pick and choose 仔細慎選**

  As you've got some job offers, you can *pick and choose* then go for the best one. 你既然有幾個工作機會，你可以仔細慎選，去做最好的。

- **come rain or shine 無論如何**

  Come rain or shine, we will definitely go camping. Even the typhoon won't stop us. 無論如何，我們絕對要去露營。連颱風都阻止不了我們。

Recently Mrs. King feels that she's ________ and is looking for help to take care of her house.

Ⓐ getting on a bit

Ⓑ making the most of

Ⓒ up and running

Could you do me a favor ________ my bag while I am in the rest room?

Ⓐ turning off

Ⓑ keeping an eye on

Ⓒ wrapping up

解答 089

解答 **(A) getting on a bit 上了年紀**

最近金太太覺得自己有點上了年紀，想要找一個幫手整理家裡。

選項 (A)getting on a bit 上了年紀 (B)making the most of 做最佳利用 (C)up and running 開始運作

補充例句

▸ **make the most of 做最佳利用**

We'll *make the most of* this fine day. We'll probably start with a walk in the wood, and then lie on the beach to relax. 我們要將這美好的一天好好利用。也許可以先到林子裡走走，然後躺在海邊休息。

▸ **up and running 開始運作**

We're working on the new computer system and hopefully it will be *up and running* by end this month. 我們正在運作新的電腦系統，希望它在這個月底就可以上線啟用。

解答 090

解答 **(B) keeping an eye on 注意，照顧**

你可以幫個忙，在我去洗手間的時候顧一下我的包包嗎？

選項 (A)turning off 關掉 (B)keeping and eye on 注意，照顧 (C)wrapping up 總結

補充例句

▸ **turn off 關掉**

Please make sure all the lights are *turned off* before you leave the classroom. 在你離開教室前，請確定所有的燈都關掉了。

▸ **wrap up 總結**

Since I won't be able to talk to you in person, let's *wrap* things *up* over the phone. 既然我不能跟你碰面說話，讓我們在電話中討論個總結。

Though I ________, I still couldn't find that pile of documents. Did you see where I put it?

A ran an errand

B took a look at

C searched high and low

We didn't do it on purpose to cause any delay on the shipment, but we'll certainly ________ your loss.

A come up against

B make up for

C vouch for

解答 091

解答 **(C) searched high and low 翻箱倒櫃**

即使我翻箱倒櫃也找不到那疊文件。你有看見我把它放到哪裡嗎？

選項 (A)ran an errand 跑腿 (B)took a look at 看一看 (C)searched high and low 翻箱倒櫃

補充例句

- **run an errand 跑腿**
  When I was a child, I liked to *run errands* for my mother because I could get out of the house. 當我還是孩子時，很喜歡幫媽媽跑腿，因為這樣就可以出門了。
- **take a look at 看一看**
  Mrs. King, would you please *take a look at* the latest itinerary and see if the arrangement is fine with you? 金女士，您可以看一下這份最新的行程表，看看這個安排適合您嗎？

解答092

解答 **(B) make up for 補償**

我們並非故意造成貨物的延誤，可是我們絕對會補償你們的損失。

選項 (A)come up against 面臨困難 (B)make up for 補償 (C)vouch for 保證

補充例句

- **come up against 面臨困境**
  The company has *come up against* serious cost cutting problems; they'll probably have to lay off some employees. 公司正面臨嚴重的降低成本問題，他們可能需要裁員。
- **vouch for 保證**
  Would you *vouch for* the fact that this is an authentic Rolex watch you're selling to me? 你可以保證你現在賣給我的勞力士錶是真品嗎？

At the moment, all roads coming downtown are running ________, please be patient and drive safely.

A bumper-to-bumper

B hand over fist

C twists and turns

Tim was ________ on a pad while the boss was talking to him about his new project.

A spilling out of

B jotting down notes

C taking it easy

解答 093

解答 **(A) bumper-to-bumper 非常擁擠**

所有進城的道路目前都是非常擁擠的，請有耐心，並且小心開車。

選項 (A)bumper-to-bumper 非常擁擠 (B)hand over fist 大量地 (C)twists and turns 迂迴曲折

補充例句

▸ **hand over fist 大量地**

One of my friends who's running her own business is making a big success and in fact, he's making money *hand over fist*. 我的一個朋友經營自己的生意很成功，而且事實上，她正在賺大錢。

▸ **twists and turns 迂迴曲折**

The movie we saw yesterday was quite amuzing and the plot had some *twists and turns* that kept the audience interested. 我們昨天看的電影很好看，迂迴曲折的情節讓觀眾興致不減。

解答 094

解答 **(B) jotting down notes 記筆記**

提姆在老闆跟他說他的新案子時在筆記本上記筆記。

選項 (A)spilling out of 灑出來 (B)jotting down notes 記筆記 (C)taking it easy 放輕鬆

補充例句

▸ **spill out of 灑出來**

The girl let some coke *spill out of* the can while she was running to her mother. 這個女孩在跑去她媽媽那裡時把可樂從罐子裡灑了出來。

▸ **take it easy 放輕鬆**

If you really want to pass your exam; I suggest that you *take it easy* first and don't panic. 如果你真的要通過考試，我建議你要先放輕鬆，不要驚慌。

Everybody is ________ something at this moment, so you'll have to wait for a while and someone will be with you.

(A) **fallen apart**

(B) **made use of**

(C) **tied up with**

During rush hours, you can see cars passing by the main street ________ .

(A) **at a distance**

(B) **out of mission**

(C) **one after another**

解答 095

解答 **(C) tied up with 忙碌於**

現在每個人都在忙，你必須等一會兒，就會有人來幫你。

選項 (A)fallen apart 破碎，崩潰 (B)made use of 利用 (C)tied up with 忙碌於

補充例句

- **fall apart** 破碎，崩潰

That old building is *falling apart* and we can't even find its main entrance. 那個老舊建築就要崩塌了，我們甚至找不到它的主要入口。

- **make use of** 利用

That smart little boy is *making use of* the box as a drum. 那個聰明的小男孩利用一個盒子當鼓。

解答 096

解答 **(C) one after another 一個接一個**

在尖峰時間，你可以在主要幹道上看見車子一輛接著一輛開過去。

選項 (A)at a distance 有一段距離 (B)out of mission 停用 (C)one after another 一個接一個

補充例句

- **at a distance** 有一段距離

The coach asked us to stand *at a distance* from each so we can exercise freely. 教練叫我們彼此保持一點距離，這樣練習時才可以自由伸展。

- **out of mission** 停用

Because the MRT is currently *out of mission*, I'll have to take the bus to work today. 因為目前捷運停駛，我今天必須搭公車上班。

Do you happen to know where this road ________? I think I'm lost.

Ⓐ **led up to**

Ⓑ **cut across**

Ⓒ **is knocked over**

Since the office now is short-staffed, most employees here are ________.

Ⓐ **squeezing in**

Ⓑ **doing double duty**

Ⓒ **going out of business**

解答 097

解答 **(A) led up to 通往**

你恰巧知道這條路通到哪裡嗎？我好像迷路了。

選項 (A)led up to 通往 (B)cut across 經過 (C)is knocked over 被撞倒，被打翻

補充例句

- **cut across 經過**
  This river *cuts across* two big ranges and sometimes their animals rest near the river. 這條河經過兩個大農莊，有時候農莊的動物會在河邊棲息。
- **be knocked over 被撞倒，被打翻**
  That trash can *was knocked over* by a reckless student, and he now needs to clean up the mess. 那個垃圾桶被一個莽撞的學生打翻了，他現在要清理這個髒亂。

解答 098

解答 **(B) doing double duty 身兼兩職**

由於公司現在人手短缺，大部分員工都身兼兩職。

選項 (A)squeezing in 強行擠進 (B)doing double duty 身兼兩職 (C)going out of business 關門，歇業

補充例句

- **squeeze in 強行擠進**
  There are so many people trying to *squeeze in* the MRT that the door almost couldn't close. 有太多人想要擠進捷運裡，所以門幾乎關不上。
- **go out of business 關門，歇業**
  Did you hear that barbecue place *went out of business* last month? I really liked their food. 你聽說那間燒烤店上個月關門了嗎？我真的很喜歡他們的食物。

That dress really ________. Can I try it on?

A shakes off

B makes public

C catches my eye

Trista asked me to ________ her tomorrow, but I can't. Can you help her out this time?

A hang out

B fill in for

C think over

解答 099

解答 **(C) catches my eye 吸引我的目光**

這件套裝真吸引我。可以讓我試穿一下嗎？

選項 (A)shakes off 痊癒 (B)makes public 公開 (C)catches my eye 吸引我的目光

補充例句

▸ **shake off 痊癒**

I wonder when I can *shake off* this lenthy cold. I'm really tired of coughing all day. 不知何時我這個拖了好久的感冒才會好。我真受不了整天咳嗽。

▸ **make public 公開**

Nancy doesn't want to *make public* of her plan of working abroad. She wants to talk to her family about this first. 南茜還不想公開她要出國工作的計畫。她想先跟家人談一談。

解答 100

解答 **(B) fill in for 代班**

崔斯塔請我明天幫她代班，可是我不行。你可以幫她忙嗎？

選項 (A)hang out 消磨時間 (B)fill in for 代班 (C)think over 仔細思考

補充例句

▸ **hang out 消磨時間**

Do you want to *hang out* together tomorrow? The exam is over and we should get out and have some fun. 你明天想要一起出去消磨時間嗎？考完試了，我們應該出去輕鬆一下。

▸ **think over 仔細思考**

You may want to *think over* before you take over that hectic work. 在接下那份忙碌的工作之前，你可能會想要仔細思考一下。

Mellisa, I'm afraid to tell you that your proposal really ________ to me. Thanks for your work any way.

A kicks off

B works out

C makes no sense

Here you go, Frank, keep this budget safe for tomorrow's board meeting. You'll ________ if you lose it.

A be in hot water

B be in short order

C be in the black

解答 101

解答 **(C) makes no sense 不合理**

梅莉莎，很抱歉告訴你，你的提案我覺得並不合理。還是謝謝你的努力。

選項 (A)kicks off 開始 (B)works out 可行，可用 (C)makes no sense 不合理

補充例句

▸ **kick off 開始**

When do we plan to *kick off* our new campaign? Is everything on schedule now? 我們的新廣告什麼時候開始？一切都跟上進度嗎？

▸ **work out 可行，可用**

After weeks of hard work, unfortunately the computer system we came up with didn't *work out*. 在數週的努力工作之後，很遺憾的，我們做出來的電腦系統並不能用。

解答 102

解答 **(A) be in hot water 有麻煩**

給你，法蘭克，把這份明天董事會要用的預算收好。如果弄丟了，你就有麻煩了。

選項 (A)be in hot water 有麻煩 (B)be in short order 迅速地 (C)be in the black 有盈餘

補充例句

▸ **in short order 迅速地**

Even though we need to have things done here *in short order*, we don't want anything to go wrong. 雖然我們要迅速地完成，但我們也不希望出錯。

▸ **in the black 有盈餘**

We're happy that our company is finally *in the black*. We've been through at least five years of down time before this. 我們很高興公司終於有盈餘了。在此之前，我們有五年的狀況都不好。

We're ________ unless we come to an agreement on how we're gonna handle this.

A getting the ball rolling

B getting our act together

C getting nowhere

We don't usually visit my grandparents. It happens ________. The last time I guess was a year ago.

A around the clock

B every now and then

C on the safe side

解答 103

解答 **(C) getting nowhere 毫無進展**

除非我們對如何進行達成協議，不然我們真的會毫無進展。

選項 (A)getting the ball rolling 開始進行 (B)getting our act together 有系統，井井有條地 (C)getting nowhere 毫無進展

補充例句

▸ **get the ball rolling 開始進行**

I've done my part but they insist on receiving order from you to *get the ball rolling*. 我已經盡了我的本分，可是他們堅持要得到你的命令才開始進行。

▸ **get one's act together 有系統，井井有條地**

In order to *get our act together*, we've bought bunches of new furniture. 為了讓我們看來井井有條，我們買了些新的家具。

解答 104

解答 **(B) every now and then 偶爾**

我們不常探訪祖父母。偶爾才去一次。上次我記得是一年前了。

選項 (A)around the clock 二十四小時連續不斷地 (B)every now and then 偶爾 (C)on the safe side 謹慎為上

補充例句

▸ **around the clock 二十四小時連續不斷地**

The café down the street opens *around the clock* and it allows us to have hot coffee in the middle of the night. 街上那間咖啡廳是二十四小時營業，所以即使半夜我們也有熱咖啡喝。

▸ **on the safe side 謹慎為上**

To be *on the safe side*, we should do research thoroughly before we make any move. 謹慎為上，我們在採取任何行動前要先仔細研究。

Roger told me that he ________ go back to the school.

A sits tight

B goes way beyond

C has half a mind to

Tell me what you want for your birthday. I'll definitely get it for you even it ________.

A costs an arm and a leg

B pops out

C catches your fancy

解答 105

解答 **(C) has half a mind to 可能會做**
羅傑告訴我，他可能回學校上課。

選項 (A)sits tight 耐心等待 (B)goes way beyond 遠超過 (C)has half a mind to可能會做

補充例句

▸ **sit tight 耐心等待**
Since we haven't heard anything from the search group, we'll have to *sit tight* and hope for the best. 既然我們還沒有得到搜救隊的任何消息，我們必須耐心等待，希望有好消息。

▸ **go way beyond 遠超過**
What you're asking here really *goes way beyond* my ability. I guess I can't help this time. 你要求的遠超過我的能力。我想這次我幫不上忙。

解答 106

解答 **(A) costs an arm and a leg 非常昂貴**
告訴我你生日要什麼。即使很昂貴，我也一定會送你。

選項 (A)costs an arm and a leg 非常昂貴 (B)pops out 不經意說出口 (C)catches your fancy 吸引你的目光

補充例句

▸ **pop out 不經意說出口**
I didn't mean to say that; it just *popped out*. I'm sorry if that made you uncomfortable. 我不是有意說的，是不經意說出口的。如果讓你不舒服，我很抱歉。

▸ **catch one's fancy 吸引某人的目光**
Nothing in this store *catches my fancy*. Shall we go to another store? 這間店沒有我喜歡的東西。我們可以去別間嗎？

I was told, ________, that John Delly is going to be transferred to New York next month.

A behind the wheel

B off the record

C have a yearning for

Something came up and I think I'll ________ for our dinner date. Sorry.

A have a rain check

B go by the book

C go for the record

解答 107

解答 **(B) off the record 私底下**

我私底下被告知，約翰戴利下個月會被調職到紐約。

選項 (A)behind the wheel 駕駛中 (B)off the record 私底下 (C)have a yearning for 渴望，盼望

補充例句

▸ **behind the wheel 駕駛中**

Aren't you *behind the wheel* now? It's dangerous to talk while driving. 你不是正在開車嗎？邊開車邊講話很危險。

▸ **have a yearning for 渴望，盼望**

I've always *had a yearning for* living in a small cottage in the countryside. 我一直渴望住在鄉間的小木屋裡。

解答 108

解答 **(A) have a rain check 改期，下次再說**

有事情發生了，所以我們今晚的晚餐約會要改期了。抱歉！

選項 (A)have a rain check 改期，下次再說 (B)by the book 照章行事 (C)for the record 正式地(說)

補充例句

▸ **by the book 照章行事**

We do things here *by the book*, so don't mess up with it, young man. 我們這裡一切照章行事，所以不要違規，年輕人。

▸ **for the record 正式地(說)**

For the record, my boss isn't too happy with your performance and has decided to terminate our partnership. 正式地告知你，我們老闆對你們的表現並不滿意，而且已經決定要終止跟你們的合作關係。

Who's the person ________ here? I need to talk to the man and get things straight with him.

A takes on

B lends a hand

C calls the shots

My attitude is firm that I'll ________ with the planned sales program. Here I officially call for your assistance and support.

A blow in

B stay course

C take issue with

解答 109

解答 **(C) calls the shots 發號施令**

這裡發號施令的人是誰？我要跟這個人把事情講清楚。

選項 (A)takes on 僱用 (B)lends a hand 幫忙 (C)calls the shots 發號施令

補充例句

▸ **take on 僱用**

Holiday sales is on the corner. We'll need to *take on* some part-time workers to help out. 假日拍賣快到了。我們需要僱用一些兼職員工來幫忙。

▸ **lend a hand 幫忙**

Could you *lend* me *a hand* when I move next month? 下個月我搬家時你可以幫忙嗎？

解答 110

解答 **(B) stay course 堅持到底**

我支持計畫好的業務計畫的態度是沒有變的。我在這裡正式呼籲你們支持和協助。

選項 (A)blow in 突然造訪 (B)stay course 堅持到底 (C)take issue with 爭論，唱反調

補充例句

▸ **blow in 突然造訪**

Luther *blew in* and surprised us last Saturday. We were so happy to see him and we got to spend that evening catching up. 路瑟上週六突然造訪，讓我們很驚喜。我們好開心見到他，而且整晚聊天敘舊。

▸ **take issue with 爭論，唱反調**

I am not here to *take issue with* you. However, I do think we need to look into this matter when we have time. 我不是來這裡跟你爭論的。不過，我真的覺得我們有空時要好好調查一下這件事。

Ever since Lisa's kids got into school, she's ________ over their troubles with their learning difficulties.

- A ahead of the times
- B on top of the world
- C torn her hair out

I'm not sure if we have enough ingredients for this recipe, but we'll ________ what we have on hand first and see what happens.

- A make do
- B be in a row
- C cut out for

解答 111

解答 **(C) torn her hair out 非常焦慮，擔心**

自從莉莎的小孩開始唸書後，她一直因為他們的學習障礙而焦慮。

選項 (A)ahead of the times 有前瞻性的 (B)on top of the world 開心至極 (C)torn her hair out 非常焦慮，擔心

補充例句

▸ **ahead of the times 有前瞻性的**

Martin Luther King was a great revolutionist whose concept was *ahead of the times*. 馬丁路德是位偉大的改革者，他的概念是有前瞻性的。

▸ **on top of the world 開心至極**

When Nate heard that his daughter got into Harvard, he felt like he was *on top of the world*. 當耐特得知他女兒進入哈佛時，他高興極了。

解答 112

解答 **(A) make do 將就，過得去**

我不確定我們是否有這個食譜所需的足夠材料，不過我們就用手邊有的，再看看會怎樣。

選項 (A)make do 將就，過得去 (B)be in a row 一連串 (C)cut out for 適合於

補充例句

▸ **in a row 一連串**

Wow! This is the fifth time *in a row* I bump into you in this neighborhood. Isn't it amazing? 哇！這是我在這一區連續第五次巧遇你了。真是太有趣了，不是嗎？

▸ **cut out for 適合於**

Nathan is really not *cut out for* receiving new customers. He's so on edge in front of them. 那森真的很不適合接待新客戶。他在他們面前真的很緊張。

You'll need to skip your lunch and get going, son. You're ________ time.

(A) **on the nose**

(B) **word has it**

(C) **short on**

Have you heard what Kenneth's ________ lately? He wouldn't tell me anything about it.

(A) **been on purpose**

(B) **been up to**

(C) **been done with**

解答 113

解答 **(C) short on 缺乏**

你必須不吃午餐直接出門了，兒子。你時間不夠了。

選項 (A)on the nose 準確，準時的 (B)word has it 聽說 (C)short on 缺乏

補充例句

- **on the nose 準確，準時的**

  Let me emphasize again, I'd like to see everybody here in the meeting room tomorrow *on the nose* at 8:00 sharp. 再次強調，我明天早上八點整要在會議室準時看到每一個人。

- **word has it 聽說**

  Word has it that the teacher who's subbing for Mr. Lin is actually going to take over his class. 聽說目前幫林老師代課的老師其實是要接他的班的。

解答 114

解答 **(B) been up to 進行，計畫**

你有聽說最近肯尼斯在計畫些什麼嗎？他什麼都不肯告訴我。

選項 (A)been on purpose 故意的 (B)been up to 進行，計畫 (C)been done with 結束，完成

補充例句

- **on purpose 故意的**

  I swear I didn't do it *on purpose*. Please believe me that it will never happen again. 我發誓我不是故意這麼做的。請相信我，不會再發生了。

- **be done with 結束，完成**

  I'*m* not *done with* you yet, young man. Don't ever think you'll get out of this after the mess you caused during the assembly. 我還沒跟你說完，年輕人。你在早上集會時造成混亂，別以為可以逃掉責任。

_______ using the elevator, I always take the stairs to go to my office on the 5th floor because I like to exercise.

Ⓐ Instead of

Ⓑ Sooner or later

Ⓒ By accident

Our new office is now _______, so we need to use this hotel room as our temporary work station for now.

Ⓐ taking pride in

Ⓑ turning out

Ⓒ in the works

解答 115

解答 **(A) Instead of 不是，而是**

我通常走樓梯到我五樓的辦公室而不搭電梯，因為我喜歡運動。

選項 (A)Instead of 不是，而是 (B)Sooner or later 遲早 (C)By accident 不小心地，意外地

補充例句

- **sooner or later 遲早**

  Sonner or later you will realize your parents always try to protect you even though they're sometimes a little harsh on you. 你遲早會了解，父母親所做的一切都是為了保護你，即使他們有時很嚴厲。

- **by accident 不小心地，意外地**

  I don't think you broke the vase *by accident*. Did you just throw ball in the living room? 我不認為你是意外打破花瓶的。你是不是在客廳丟球？

解答 116

解答 **(C) in the works 正在準備或進行**

我們的新辦公室正在籌備，所以我們目前需要用這間飯店房間作為臨時工作的地方。

選項 (A)taking pride in 對…感到自豪或光榮 (B)turning out 結果是 (C)in the works 正在準備或進行

補充例句

- **take pride in 對…感到自豪或光榮**

  Julia really *takes pride in* her children's outstanding achievements. They're both well-known doctors in the States. 茱莉亞對她孩子的傑出成就感到光榮。他們現在都是美國知名的醫生。

- **turn out 結果是**

  After all the efforts we put in for the past few months, the project *turned out* to be a big disaster. What a shame! 在我們過去幾個月的努力之後，這個案子最後竟然變成災難收場。真丟臉！

There's still time before the train leaves. What do you say we ________ in that diner next to the station? I'm a little hungry.

A **are on leave**

B **have a bite**

C **live out of a suitcase**

It's really amazing that you can ________ his bad temper. I can't even talk to him for more than 1 minute.

A **put up with**

B **break up**

C **put your weight**

解答 117

解答 **(B) have a bite 吃點東西**

火車離開前還有時間。你覺得我們去火車站旁邊那間餐廳吃點東西如何？我有點餓了。

選項 (A)are on leave 休假 (B)have a bite 吃點東西 (C)live out of a suitcase 因旅行住在旅館

補充例句

▸ **on leave 休假**

I'm afraid that the person in charge is *on leave* today. You may have to come back again tomorrow. 抱歉，負責的人今天休假。你可能要明天再跑一趟。

▸ **live out of a suitcase 因旅行住在旅館**

Due to Mr. Lucas' traveling a lot on business, he says he's *living out of a suitcase* all year round. 因為盧卡司先生經常出差旅行，他說他經年累月都得住在旅館。

解答 118

解答 **(A) put up with 忍受**

你能夠忍受他的脾氣真是很不可思議。我幾乎無法跟他說話超過一分鐘。

選項 (A)put up with 忍受 (B)break up 通話中斷 (C)put your weight 盡職，盡本分

補充例句

▸ **break up 通話中斷**

I can't hear you, Timmy. It seems that the phone line's been *breaking up*. 我聽不見你說話，提米。電話線好像中斷了。

▸ **put one's weight 盡職，盡本分**

As long as everyone *puts their weight*, the situation will turn around for sure. 只要每個人都盡本分，狀況一定會好轉的。

You're always ________ at lunch. No wonder you always have a stomachache.

A on your way home

B on the run

C put your feet up

After talking to the doctor, Joan finally ________ on the symptoms she's been having.

A called in sick

B knew the score

C sorted out

解答 119

解答 **(B) on the run 匆匆忙忙**

你總是在午餐時匆匆忙忙，難怪你會胃痛。

選項 (A)on your way home 在回家的途中 (B)on the run 匆匆忙忙 (C)put your feet up 放輕鬆

補充例句

▸ **on one's way home 在回家的途中**

Rachel saw a hugry kitten *on her way home*. She bought her some milk and brought it home. She hoped that she could keep it. 瑞秋在回家途中看到一隻飢餓的小貓。她買牛奶給牠喝，並帶牠回家。她希望可以養牠。

▸ **put one's feet up 放輕鬆**

The doctor suggest that I *put my feet up* once in a while, and then I'll feel a lot better and my headache will soon be away. 醫生建議我有時可以放輕鬆，那麼我就會感覺好多了，頭痛也會痊癒。

解答 120

解答 **(B) knew the score 了解狀況**

在跟醫生談過之後，瓊終於了解她身體的症狀。

選項 (A)called in sick 打電話請病假 (B)knew the score 了解狀況 (C)sorted out 整理

補充例句

▸ **call in sick 打電話請病假**

I was surprised that Randy *called in sick*. Randy is the person who shows up for work even she's having a fever. 我很驚訝蘭蒂打電話請病假。蘭蒂是那種即使發燒也會出現的人。

▸ **sort out 整理**

It took me like a whole week to *sort out* the problems of my stereo and now it's finally fixed. 我花了一整個星期整理出音響的問題，現在終於修好了。

Honey, it's time to get going. Did you find anything that ________ here?

A fits the bill

B turns your head

C keeps track of

It's really ________ doing the same thing over and over again just because the boss wants us to do.

A inside and out

B pros and cons of

C a pain in the neck

解答 121

解答 **(A) fit the bill 符合目的**

親愛的，該走了哦！你有找到合意的東西嗎？

選項 (A)fit the bill 符合目的 (B)turn your head 讓你開心、興奮 (C)keep track of 注意

補充例句

- **turn one's head 讓人開心、興奮**

Our new commercial works really well. It really *turns people's heads* when it's on TV. 我們的新廣告很有效。在電視上播出時，真的讓很多人很開心。

- **keep track of 注意**

Wanda *keeps track of* all her belongings when she travels, especially her passport and money. 汪達在旅行時很注意她的隨身物品，尤其是她的護照和錢。

解答 122

解答 **(C) a pain in the neck 令人煩惱或生氣的事**

因為老闆希望我們如此做，我們就得重複做同樣的事，真是讓人生氣。

選項 (A)inside and out 完全地，徹底地 (B)pros and cons of 利與弊 (C)a pain in the neck 令人煩惱或生氣的事

補充例句

- **inside and out 完全地，徹底地**

Annett was really upset about the mistakes in her book. She thought she checked it *inside and out* thoroughly and apparently she could have been more cautious. 安奈特對於她書中的錯誤很難過。她以為她已經檢查得很徹底了，而顯然地她其實可以更仔細。

- **pros and cons of 利與弊**

Have you discussed all the *pros and cons of* these two possible promotion plans? Are you ready to tell me which one you have decided to adopt? 你們針對這兩個可能的促銷方案的利弊都討論過了嗎？你們準備好告訴我決定要採用哪一個了嗎？

Would you please turn down that music? That noise is ________.

A free for the taking

B music to my ears

C driving me nuts

I heard there's a typhoon on its way. We'd better ________ the weather report on the radio to get to know the latest situation.

A keep an ear on

B take place

C do our bit

解答 123

解答 **(C) driving me nuts 讓我發瘋**

你可以把音樂關小聲嗎？那噪音讓我快發瘋了。

選項 (A)free for the taking 自由使用 (B)music to my ears 好消息 (C)driving me nuts 讓我發瘋

補充例句

▸ **free for the taking 自由使用**

Be careful when you adopt information from the internet. Most information is protected by copyright and not *free for the taking*. 當你使用網路資訊時要小心。大部分資料都是有版權保護的，不可以自由使用。

▸ **music to one's ears 好消息**

It's *music to my ears* when Dawson told me that he's gonna fix my kitchen sink today. 當道森告訴我今天可以幫我修廚房水槽時，真是個好消息。

解答 124

解答 **(A) keep an ear on 注意聽**

我聽說有個颱風要來。我們最好注意聽電臺的氣象報告，才知道最新情況。

選項 (A)keep an ear on 注意聽 (B)take place 舉行，發生 (C)do our bit 做分內的事

補充例句

▸ **take place 舉行，發生**

This time's International Floral Expo is *taking place* in Taipei and people from all over the world are here for it. 這次的花博在臺北舉行，世界各國的人都因此而來。

▸ **do one's bit 做分內的事**

Everyone in this family should *do their bit*, don't you think? It's not only the parents' responsibility to clean the house. 你不認為家中每個人都該盡本分嗎？整理家裡不該只是父母的責任。

Look, we're in the hospital visiting your grandmother. I know you're concerned about your work, but please ________ taking any cell phone calls.

Ⓐ **by all means**

Ⓑ **hang on**

Ⓒ **refrain from**

On the weekends, I usually go out with friends. But my sister who's ________ always stays home and never goes out.

Ⓐ **under a cloud**

Ⓑ **fair and square**

Ⓒ **the other way around**

解答 125

解答 **(C) refrain from 抑制，忍住**

聽好，我們現在在醫院探望你祖母。我知道你很關心工作，可是請你不要接聽手機。

選項 (A)by all means 務必，想盡辦法 (B)hang on 不要掛斷電話 (C)refrain from 抑制，忍住

補充例句

▸ **by all means 務必，想盡辦法**

We've been planning on opening this restaurant for years. *By all means*, we'll stick to the plan and make it happen. 我們計畫要開這間餐廳好多年了。我們想盡辦法也要讓這件事成功。

▸ **hang on 不要掛斷電話**

You want to talk with Mr. Evans? *Hang on*. Let me see if he is around here for you. 你要跟伊凡斯先生說話嗎？別掛電話，讓我看看他有沒有在這裡。

解答 126

解答 **(C) the other way around 恰好相反**

週末我都會跟朋友出去。可是我的姊姊完全相反，她總是待在家裡，從不出門。

選項 (A)under a cloud 受到懷疑 (B)fair and square 公正的，光明正大的 (C)the other way around 恰好相反

補充例句

▸ **under a cloud 受到懷疑**

Ever since stories of beating children at this day-care center apeared, it has been *under a cloud* and lost a lot of students. 自從這間安親班會打人的事件發生後，它就被大家懷疑，而且失去不少學生。

▸ **fair and square 公正的，光明正大的**

As a member of the evaluation team, I can assure you that the process is *fair and square* to everyone. 身為評量小組的一員，我可以跟你保證，所有過程都是公正無私的。

Just the day before Carolyn's wedding, she ________ and ran away. Tim felt hurt, but he said he didn't blame her.

A **went broke**

B **got cold feet**

C **got together**

Don't tell me you're doing your homework. No one could read with a book ________.

A **upside down**

B **up and down**

C **up in the air**

解答 127

解答 **(B) got cold feet** 害怕，失去信心

在卡洛琳婚禮的前一天，她因害怕而逃走了。提姆很受傷，但是他說他不怪她。

選項 (A)went broke 破產 (B)got cold feet 害怕，失去信心 (C)got together 聚會

補充例句

▸ **go broke** 破產

If you don't use your credit card carefully, you may *go broke* when you don't have money to pay back the bank. 如果你不謹慎使用信用卡，當你沒有錢還銀行的時候，你可能會破產。

▸ **get together** 聚會

Back in high school, we usually *got together* at the tea house near our school after class. 高中時，我們下課後通常會在學校附近那間茶館聚會。

解答 128

解答 **(A) upside down** 上下顛倒

別跟我說你在做功課。沒有人可以顛倒看書的。

選項 (A)upside down 上下顛倒 (B)up and down 上上下下，來來回回 (C)up in the air 懸而未決

補充例句

▸ **up and down** 上上下下，來來回回

My father works as a delivery staff at Pizza Hut. He needs to drive *up and down* all day. 我父親在必勝客送披薩。他整天都要開車來來回回。

▸ **up in the air** 懸而未決

Whether we'll be able to get our annual bonus is still *up in the air*. The boss says they need to take everything into consideration before making the decision. 我們是否會有年終獎金還不確定。老闆說要全面考慮後再做決定。

Our surpervisor urged us to complete our assignment ________ because the director may blow in any time today.

A run its course

B take part in

C on the double

Being an actress in Samantha's family is ______. Her parents want her to be either a teacher or a nurse.

A free and easy

B giving it a try

C out of bounds

解答 129

解答 **(C) on the double 快速地**

我們的主任叫我們快點把工作做完，因為處長今天隨時會來視察。

選項 (A) run its course 痊癒，順其自然 (B)take part in 參加 (C)on the double 快速地

補充例句

- **run its course 痊癒，順其而然**

Instead of letting the flu *run its course*, the doctors suggest that we all take the flu shots. 醫生建議我們要打流行感冒預防針，不要讓感冒自然痊癒。

- **take part in 參加**

People who *take part in* answering the questionnaire are aged from 25 to 40. 參加這份問卷調查的人年齡在25歲到40歲之間。

解答 130

解答 **(C) out of bounds 不允許的**

在莎曼莎家中當演員是不允許的。她的父母希望她當老師或護士。

選項 (A)free and easy 毫無拘束的 (B)giving it a try 試試看 (C)out of bounds 不允許的

補充例句

- **free and easy 毫無拘束的**

In order to make your life *free and easy*, now you can find our service in every convenience store in your neighborhood. 為了讓您的生活更便利，您現在可以在家附近所有的便利商店得到我們的服務。

- **give it a try 試試看**

They told me that the new restaurant is really nice. Why don't we *give it a try* tonight? We're eating out anyway. 他們告訴我那間新餐廳很不錯。我們今晚去試試看吧？反正我們要出去吃飯。

________ the unreasonable high living cost, Jonathan and his wife decided to move out of the city and commute to work.

A Sticking with

B Being fed up with

C Taking effect

Amber not only always ________ the company requirements, but never showed up at work on time. As a result, he got demoted.

A bit the dust

B bothered with

C lost track of

解答 131

解答 **(B) Being fed up with 對…感到厭煩**

因為對高生活成本感到厭煩，強納森夫婦決定搬出市區，通車上班。

選項 (A)Sticking with 持續 (B)Being fed up with 對…感到厭煩 (C)Taking effect 見效，開始實施

補充例句

- **stick with 持續**

  The director asks us to plan a work schedule and *stick with* it. 處長要求我們做出工作時程表，然後持續照表操課。

- **take effect 見效，開始實施**

  This drug won't *take effect* until two hours after taking. 這個藥要在吃下去兩個小時之後才會見效。

解答 132

解答 **(C) lost track of 不清楚**

安博不只老搞不清楚公司的要求，還不準時上班。結果他被降職了。

選項 (A)bit the dust 被打敗，陣亡 (B)bothered with 為…煩心 (C)lost track of 不清楚

補充例句

- **bite the dust 被打敗，陣亡**

  If you want all your troubles to *bite the dust*, the first thing is that you need to face them with courage. 如果你想要所有的麻煩都不見，首先你要勇敢面對他們。

- **bother with 為…煩心**

  Don't *bother with* our travel plans. My friend working in a travel agency will have everything well planned before we leave. 不要為旅遊計畫煩心。我在旅行社工作的朋友會在我們出發前把一切搞定。

It's good to know that we've been ________ on the project. If things go on schedule, we'll be able to launch our new product by the end of this year.

Ⓐ **making good time**

Ⓑ **making time**

Ⓒ **passing the time**

Since I'm driving to work tomorrow, I can ________ on my way to the office.

Ⓐ **pick you up**

Ⓑ **take over**

Ⓒ **make your day**

解答 133

解答 **(A) making good time 進行順利**

很高興知道我們這個案子進行順利。如果一切都按照進度，我們的新產品在今年年底就可以上市了。

選項 (A)making good time 進行順利 (B)making time 騰出時間 (C)passing the time 消磨時間

補充例句

▸ **make time 騰出時間**

Chinese New Year's around the corner now. We ought to *make time* to clean up the house and do some holiday shopping. 農曆新年快到了，我們該找時間整理家裡，做些採買了。

▸ **pass the time 消磨時間**

What do you suggest we do now to *pass the time*? There's some time before boarding and we've got no place to go. 你建議我們現在要做些什麼來殺時間？登機前還有些時間，且我們也沒有地方可以去。

解答 134

解答 **(A) pick you up 接你**

既然我明天要開車上班，我可以順道接你。

選項 (A)pick you up 接你 (B)take over 接管，接收 (C)make your day 讓你非常高興

補充例句

▸ **take over 接收，接管**

My wife's not happy with the fact that I was asked to *take over* Timothy's job and transffered to Seattle. That means we'll need to move again. 我太太對於我要接收提摩西的職位，調到西雅圖很不開心，因為那表示我們又要搬家了。

▸ **make one's day 讓人非常高興**

The kids *made my day* by telling me that I'm the best mother in the world. 孩子們告訴我我是世界上最好的媽媽時讓我非常高興。

The audience ________ when the speaker was telling the secret of making a big fortune in the stock market.

A **put away**

B **were all ears**

C **dropped in**

Let's ________ and make some room for Sharon.

A **move over**

B **break out**

C **think twice**

解答 135

解答 **(B) were all ears 仔細聆聽**

當演講者在告訴大家在股市賺大錢的祕訣時，觀眾都仔細聆聽。

選項 (A)put away 拋棄，丟掉 (B)were all ears 仔細聆聽 (C)dropped in 順道拜訪

補充例句

- **put away 拋棄，丟掉**

Would you please *put away* those used boxes outside the house? The cleaner said he would come and pick them up later. 你可以把那些用過的箱子丟到房子外面嗎？清潔工說他待會兒會來拿。

- **drop in 順道拜訪**

Before I come to the party, I'll need to *drop in* at Mary's house to return the racket I borrowed from her. 我來派對前，必須經過瑪麗家把我跟她借的網球拍還給她。

解答 136

解答 **(A) move over 讓出位置**

讓我們讓出點位置給雪倫。

選項 (A)move over 讓出位置 (B)break out 爆發，流行 (C)think twice 深思熟慮

補充例句

- **break out 爆發，流行**

This year's flu has *broken out* in schools and lots of students call in sick. Some schools even have to stop classes. 今年的流行性感冒在學校裡流行，很多學生都請假。有些學校甚至必須停課。

- **think twice 深思熟慮**

In order not to say anything wrong, Judith *thinks twice* before she speaks and sometimes she just keeps silent. 為了不要說錯話，茱蒂絲說話前都會深思熟慮，而有時她只保持沉默。

The man ________ his former employer who failed to pay him salary for almost a year.

A broke the ice

B ate humble pie

C spoke ill of

Listen! Mr. Lohan is our biggest investor, so later when he arrives, I'd like you all to welcome him ________.

A on the beat

B with open arms

C in brief

解答 137

解答 **(C) spoke ill of 說…壞話**

這個人在說他的前任雇主的壞話，他前任雇主有一年沒付他薪水。

選項 (A)broke the ice 打破沉默 (B)ate humble pie 忍氣吞聲 (C)spoke ill of 說…壞話

補充例句

- **break the ice 打破沉默**

It's the students' first day and they're all shy and new here. I think I will do some games to *break the ice* and get them talking. 今天是新生第一天來這裡，他們都很害羞，我想我要玩些遊戲來打破沉默，讓他們說話。

- **eat humble pie 忍氣吞聲**

Anita knew well that it's her fault this time, so she *ate humble pie* and apoligized. 安妮塔知道這次是她的錯，所以她忍氣吞聲，並且道歉。

解答 138

解答 **(B) with open arms 熱烈地**

聽好。羅漢先生是我們最大的投資者，所以等一下他來時，我要你們全部都熱烈地歡迎他。

選項 (A)on the beat 合拍子 (B)with open arms 熱烈地 (C)in brief 簡言之

補充例句

- **on the beat 合拍子**

Now I'd like to give you one more chance. But when you sing this time, please be *on the beat*. 現在我要再給你一次機會。可是你這次唱的時候，請你要合拍子。

- **in brief 簡言之**

In brief, our sales department's been facing serious problems recently and I urge you all to offer them support and assistance. 簡言之，我們的業務部門最近一直面臨嚴重的問題，我請你們都要給他們支持與協助。

At the training center, the trainees can ________ wherever they want to go after the sesssion's over.

- A get off
- B put in place
- C move about

________ the weather problem, the traffic also makes it difficult for us to arrive on time.

- A Pull in
- B Set aside
- C In addition to

解答 139

解答 **(C) move about 隨意走動**

在訓練中心，所有的受訓員在下課後都可以隨意走動。

選項 (A)get off 下車 (B)put in place 設置，引進 (C)move about 隨意走動

補充例句

▸ **get off 下車**

For passengers going to Miramar Department Store, please *get off* at this station. 要到美麗華百貨公司的乘客，請在本站下車。

▸ **put in place 設置，引進**

After our new file cabinets *put in place*, you can start putting away your files and make the office look organized. 在我們的新檔案櫃設置好之後，你們可以開始把檔案放好，讓辦公室看來井然有序。

解答 140

解答 **(C) In addition to 除了**

除了天氣問題外，交通也是讓我們無法準時到達的原因。

選項 (A)Pull in 到達，到站 (B)Set aside 保留，撥出 (C)In addition to 除了

補充例句

▸ **pull in 到達，到站**

Don't rush. There's plenty of time before the train *pulls in*. We're totally in time. 不要急。火車到站前我們還有很多時間。我們完全趕得上。

▸ **set aside 保留，撥出**

Is it possible for you to *set aside* a few hours tomorrow for the participants to get acqainted with each other? 你可能在明天撥出幾個小時讓參與者彼此熟識嗎？

You made too many mistakes in your sales report. Please ________ and hand it in the first thing tomorrow.

A look into

B blow up

C do it over

Please ________ to use my computer while I'm away.

A feel like

B feel free

C feel funny

解答 141

解答 **(C) do it over 重做**

你的業務報告裡有太多錯誤了。請重做一份，明天第一件事就交上來。

選項 (A)look into 調查 (B)blow up 吹氣球 (C)do it over 重做

補充例句

▸ **look into 調查**

The police are *looking into* the murder case now and hopefully they will have the killer arrested soon. 警方正在調查這個謀殺案，希望他們很快可以將兇手繩之以法。

▸ **blow up 吹氣球**

How many balloons do we need to *blow up* for this party? 我們要為這個宴會吹多少個氣球呢？

解答 142

解答 **(B) feel free 不要客氣**

我不在的時候請自由使用我的電腦，不要客氣。

選項 (A)feel like 想要 (B)feel free 不要客氣 (C)feel funny 感覺不對勁

補充例句

▸ **feel like 想要**

I *feel like* eating hamburgers today. 我今天想要吃漢堡。

▸ **feel funny 感覺不對勁**

I've been *feeling funny* ever since I ate that pizza earlier today. Do you feel the same? 我今天稍早吃了那個披薩之後肚子就怪怪的。你也會這樣嗎？

While I'm away, could you ________ my baby dog? He won't cause you any trouble, I promise.

A make fun of

B look after

C be cut-and-dried

After going back to the States from Taiwan, please don't forget to ________ with us.

A stay in touch

B watch your step

C have in mind

解答 143

解答 **(B) look after 照顧**

我不在的時候你可以幫我照顧我的小狗嗎？牠不會給你找任何麻煩的，我保證。

選項 (A)make fun of 捉弄 (B)look after 照顧 (C)be cut-and-dried 可預測的

補充例句

▸ **make fun of 捉弄**

Don't *make fun of* that new comer. You're supposed to be nice and warm to him. 不要捉弄那位新朋友。你應該要對他友善，讓他感受到溫暖才是。

▸ **cut-and-dried (= predictable) 可預測的**

After being here for a year, the routine has become *cut-and-dried*. 在這裡待了一年之後，所有的例行公事都已經是可預測的了。

解答 144

解答 **(A) stay in touch 保持聯絡**

從臺灣回到美國之後，請別忘了與我們保持聯絡。

選項 (A)stay in touch 保持聯絡 (B)watch your step 小心腳步 (C)have in mind 在想…

補充例句

▸ **watch one's step 小心腳步**

That trail is not in good condition. When you walk there, please *watch your step*. 這條路狀況不好。當你走到那裡時，請小心腳步。

▸ **have in mind 在想…**

Do you *have in mind* what kind of office you're looking for? We can do whatever renovation you want. 你想要有哪一種辦公室？我們可以做出你所想的任何裝潢。

Jolin walks so fast that I can't ________ her.

A turn down

B break in

C keep up with

You'd ________ taking my advice for the job. I worked there for three months and quit because I found that they weren't nice people.

A be better off

B be well-off

C be into

解答 145

解答 **(C) keep up with 跟上**

裘琳走得太快了，我無法趕上她。

選項 (A)turn down 拒絕 (B)break in 闖入 (C)keep up with 趕上

補充例句

▸ **turn down 拒絕**

Even though she *turned down* my request, I didn't feel hurt because she must have her reason. 雖然她拒絕了我的請求，我並不覺得受傷，因為她一定有她的理由。

▸ **break in 闖入**

A thief *broke in* Lee's house last night. Fortunately, he only took things instead of hurting people. 有一個小偷昨晚闖入李的家中。幸運的是，他只有拿東西，沒有傷人。

解答 146

解答 **(A) be better off 最好**

你最好在這個工作上聽我的建議。我在那裡工作了三個月就辭職，因為我發現他們不是好人。

選項 (A)be better off 最好 (B)be well-off 富裕 (C)be into 對…有興趣

補充例句

▸ **be well-off 富裕**

Those two boys *are* from a very *well-off* family. And that's why they are spoiled and listen to no one. 那兩個男孩來自非常富裕的家庭。那就是他們被寵壞了而且誰的話也不聽的原因。

▸ **be into 對…有興趣**

I'*m* not really *into* fashion like most teenagers. Literature and art are more my style. 我不像那些青少年對時尚那麼有興趣。文學和藝術比較是我喜歡的風格。

Why should I ________ you? You've been lying to me for too many times.

A **believe in**

B **cheer up**

C **draw up**

Jack shouldn't ________ that job because he's always wanted to work in that company.

A **live up to**

B **have second thoughts about**

C **fade away**

解答 147

解答 **(A) believe in 相信**

我為什麼要相信你？你已經欺騙我非常多次了。

選項 (A)believe in 相信 (B)cheer up 鼓舞 (C)draw up 擬定

補充例句

▸ **cheer up 鼓舞**

No matter what we did to *cheer* him *up*, the little boy still didn't stop crying. 不管我們做什麼鼓舞他，這小男孩就是不停地哭。

▸ **draw up 擬定**

Have you finished *drawing up* the contract for tomorrow? The boss wants to have a look now. 你擬好明天那份合約了嗎？老闆現在想看一下。

解答 148

解答 **(B) have second thoughts about 有疑問，改變主意**

傑克不應該對那份工作有疑惑，因為他一直都想要在那間公司工作。

選項 (A)live up to 達到 (B)have second thoughts about 有疑問，改變主意 (C)fade away 褪色，淡忘

補充例句

▸ **live up to 達到**

I know I'll never *live up to* my family's expectations. I just don't want to be a solider. 我知道我永遠都達不到我的家庭對我的期望。我只是不想當軍人罷了。

▸ **fade away 褪色，淡忘**

I will not let this good memory *fade away* and I'll always remember these days. 我將不會讓這段美好的回憶褪色，我會永遠記得這些日子的。

If anything ________ here, I must be the first one to know.

A goes wrong

B sticks up

C puts in place

We had no choice but to cancel the concert because a problem with the stage just ________.

A hung up

B saw fit

C cropped up

解答 149

解答 **(A) goes wrong 出錯**

如果有任何事出錯，我一定要是第一個知道的人。

選項 (A)goes wrong 出錯 (B)sticks up 搶劫 (C)puts in place 設置，引進

補充例句

- **stick up 搶劫**

  Did you hear that the store down the street was *stuck up* by a masked man last night? 你聽說街上那間店昨晚被一個蒙面人搶了嗎？

- **put in place 設置，引進**

  Attention, please. We will start getting off the airplane when the staircase is *put in place*. Watch out your step. 請注意，我們在放好梯子後會開始下飛機。請留意您的腳步。

解答 150

解答 **(C) cropped up (問題)意外發生**

我們必須要取消演唱會，因為舞臺臨時出問題。

選項 (A)hung up 掛電話 (B)saw fit 認為恰當 (C)cropped up (問題)意外發生

補充例句

- **hang up 掛電話**

  I was really upset when you *hung up* on me yesterday. I knew you were mad but we should have talked things over instead. 昨天你掛我電話，我很傷心。我知道你生氣，可是我們應該把事情談清楚，不該掛電話。

- **see fit 認為恰當**

  I didn't *see fit* for us to wonder around in the woods alone. We don't really know this area well enough. 我不認為我們獨自在林子裡走是恰當的。我們對這一區並不夠熟識。

This project is now _______. I'd like to take this opportunity to thank the crew for their hard work in the past two years.

A covering a lot of ground

B in the homestretch

C free for the taking

Why didn't the security chip on the price tag set off when the thief _______ the goods? There must be something wrong with the chip.

A walked away with

B turned aside

C took on

解答 151

解答 **(B) in the homestretch 最後階段**

這個案子正在最後階段。我要藉這個機會感謝工作人員在過去兩年的努力。

選項 (A)covering a lot of ground 內容深入且包羅萬象 (B)in the homestretch 最後階段 (C)free for the taking 免費使用

補充例句

- **cover a lot of ground 內容深入且包羅萬象**

  This report really *covers a lot of ground*. Don't you think it really gives us a lot of different ideas? 這個報導真是深入。你不覺得它給了我們很多不同的想法嗎？

- **free for the taking 免費使用**

  Nothing here is *free for the taking*. Fortunately, they're not too expensive. 這裡沒有東西是免費的。幸運的是，東西並不太貴。

解答 152

解答 **(A) walked away with 輕易取得，偷走**

小偷偷走貨品時，價格標籤上的安全晶片怎麼沒有響呢？那個晶片一定有問題。

選項 (A)walked away with 輕易取得，偷走 (B)turned aside 避開，不理 (C)took on 採用，僱用

補充例句

- **turn aside 避開，不理**

  My daughter *turned aside* the teacher's suggestion and insisted on her own way of study. 我女兒不理會老師給她的建議，堅持用自己的方法讀書。

- **take on 採用，僱用**

  Even though we are short-staffed, the management has decided not to *take on* any more workers. 雖然我們現在人手不足，管理部仍然決定不再增聘人手。

It's good to know that our new partner ________ some new investors worldwide.

A brought to the table

B hit the books

C went for a drive

You shouldn't be ashamed of yourself because you have done your best. You should ________ and be proud of yourself.

A break new ground

B bring home

C hold your head up

解答 153

解答 **(A) brought to the table 提供**

很高興知道，我們的新夥伴提供了來自世界各地的新投資者。

選項 (A)brought to the table 提供 (B)hit the books 用功讀書 (C)went for a drive 開車兜風

補充例句

- **hit the books 用功讀書**

  As final exams are around the corner, students all *hit the books* in the library. 期末考要到了，學生都在圖書館用功讀書。

- **go for a drive 開車兜風**

  What do you say we *go for a drive* in the countryside during the holiday? We can have some fresh air there. 你覺得我們在假期中到鄉間開車兜風如何？我們可以在那裡呼吸新鮮空氣。

解答 154

解答 **(C) hold your head up 昂首，驕傲**

你不該羞愧，因為你已盡了全力。你應該抬頭挺胸，並且為自己感到驕傲。

選項 (A)break new ground 首次嘗試 (B)bring home 強烈感受，逼真呈現 (C)hold your head up 昂首，驕傲

補充例句

- **break new ground 首次嘗試**

  In the next season, we'll *break new ground* by doing the survey countrywide. It'll be our first time, and please be ready for that. 下一季，我們要首次嘗試做全國性的問卷調查。這會是我們第一次的嘗試，請大家準備好。

- **bring home 強烈感受，逼真呈現**

  This book *brings home* the story of a humble family going through their most difficult stage of life. 這本書逼真地呈現了一個貧苦家庭經歷人生中最辛苦階段的故事。

Sean is the kind of person who ________ and we always rely on him when things become tough.

A plays ball

B knows a thing or two

C makes tracks

Why do you want to be a ________? Minding your own business will save you a lot of trouble.

A you and yours

B backseat driver

C take the wheels

解答 155

解答 **(B) knows a thing or two 精明能幹**

西恩是很精明能幹的人，我們碰到難事都依賴他。

選項 (A)plays ball 動手，開始行動 (B)knows a thing or two 精明能幹 (C)makes tracks 快速行動

補充例句

- **play ball 動手，開始行動**

  It's harder than I thought to get him to *play ball*. He is such a stubborn person. 要讓他開始行動，比我想像還要難。他真是個頑固的人。

- **make tracks 快速行動**

  For customers who are interested in getting our New Year's giveaways, please *make tracks* to the customer service on the 10th floor. 對我們新年贈品有興趣的顧客，請快到十樓的客服中心。

解答 156

解答 **(B) backseat driver 愛管閒事的人**

你為什麼想要做個愛管閒事的人呢？管好自己才可以免掉很多麻煩。

選項 (A)you and yours 各位 (B)backseat driver 愛管閒事的人 (C)take the wheels 控制局面

補充例句

- **you and yours 各位**

  We're honored to have *you and yours* in our hotel, and we hope you all enjoy staying here with us. 我們感到很榮幸各位駕臨本飯店，希望你們住得愉快。

- **take the wheels 控制局面**

  Back in the sixties, Ms. Louis was the one who *took the wheels* in the company. But now she's stepped down. 回到六〇年代，路易斯女士在公司是發號施令的人，但現在她已經卸任了。

It's natural that investors want to get as much ________ as they can, so it's important to keep informed of market trends.

A hovering around

B bringing forth

C bang for the buck

You've got to trust me. Choosing the AMC to start with your career is your ________. They offer their staff good benefit and training.

A swings and roundabouts

B best bet

C better yet

解答 157

解答 **(C) bang for the buck** 回收

投資者自然希望能夠回本，所以讓他們隨時了解市場狀況很重要。

選項 (A)hovering around 上下震盪 (B)bringing forth 激發出 (C)bang for the buck 回收

補充例句

- **hover around** 上下震盪

The US unemployment rate had been *hovering around* 5% for most of the decade until there was a sharp increase toward the end. 美國的失業率過去十年大多在百分之五上下遊走，直到最後才有了劇烈的爬升。

- **bring forth** 激發出

Luckily, the President's announcement of the new agricultural policy didn't *bring forth* opposition from farmers. 幸運地，總統對新的農業政策的宣告並沒有激發農民極大的反對聲浪。

解答 158

解答 **(B) best bet** 最受推薦的事

你要相信我。選擇AMC公司開始你的事業是最好的選擇。他們提供員工最好的福利和訓練。

選項 (A)swings and roundabouts 有得必有失 (B)best bet 最受推薦的事 (C)better yet 可以的話

補充例句

- **swings and roundabouts** 有得必有失

Life is never predictable. Every choice you make will have *swings and roundabouts* and you just have to look at the positive side of it. 人生是不可預測的。你做的每一個決定都有得有失，你只需要正面看待每一件事。

- **better yet** 可以的話

School requires all students pass GEPT test before they graduate and *better yet* the intermediate level of it. 學校要求所有學生畢業前都要通過全民英檢，可以的話，最好是中級的。

After the whole afternoon of training, these basketball players all ________.

A ate like a horse

B were in hot water

C got nowhere

Have you seen my sunglasses? I've looked ________ and just couldn't find it.

A from then on

B every nook and cranny

C every so often

解答 159

解答 **(A) ate like a horse 吃很多**

在整個下午的訓練之後，這些籃球選手胃口大開。

選項 (A)ate like a horse 吃很多 (B)were in hot water 有麻煩 (C)got nowhere 沒有進展

補充例句

- **be in hot water 有麻煩**

I heard that Jessie *is* now *in hot water* because she lost the biggest client of the company and she may end up being fired. 我聽說潔西現在面臨麻煩，因為她失去公司最大的客戶，有可能會被解僱。

- **get nowhere 沒有進展**

Come on! Tell me what you think. We're *getting nowhere* if you don't say anything. 說吧！告訴我你怎麼想。如果你什麼都不說，我們是沒有進展的。

解答 160

解答 **(B) every nook and cranny 到處**

你有看到我的太陽眼鏡嗎？我到處找都沒找到。

選項 (A)from then on 從那時起 (B)every nook and cranny 到處 (C)every so often 不時，偶爾

補充例句

- **from then on 從那時起**

I met Sally at high school. *From then on*, we've been best friends for decades. 我和莎莉在高中時認識。從那時起，我們做了幾十年的好朋友。

- **every so often 不時，偶爾**

Johnny doesn't like to go shopping with me. *Every so often* he accompanies me to the department store but I know he doesn't enjoy it. 強尼不喜歡跟我去逛街，有時候他陪我去百貨公司，但我知道他並不開心。

Note

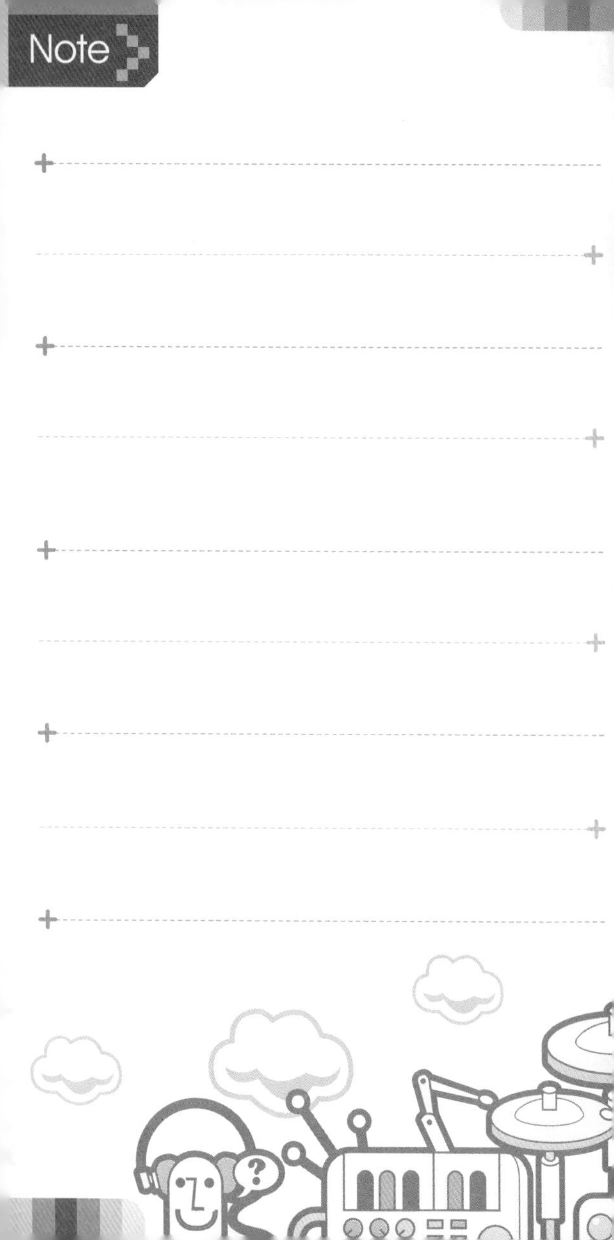
Note

Note
?

Note

Note

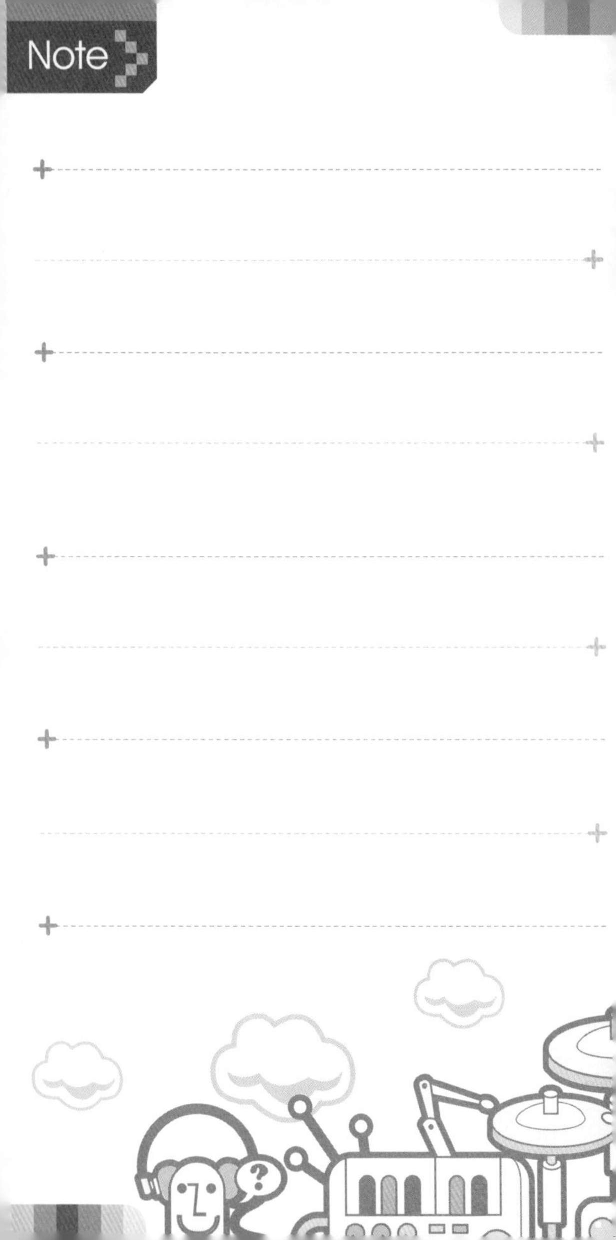

Note
?

國家圖書館出版品預行編目資料

1 日 1 分鐘新多益必考片語問題集／劉慧如, Tom Brink 編著. ——初版. ——臺北市：書泉，2012.03
面；　公分

ISBN 978-986-121-737-6（平裝附光碟片）

1. 多益測驗　2.慣用語

805. 1895　　101002033

3AN4

1 日 1 分鐘新多益必考片語問題集

作　　者　劉慧如、Tom Brink
發 行 人　楊榮川
總 編 輯　龐君豪
責任編輯　溫小瑩
版型設計　吳佳臻
封面設計　吳佳臻

出 版 者　書泉出版社
地　　址：台北市大安區 106 和平東路二段 339 號 4 樓
電　　話：(02)2705-5066（代表號）
傳　　真：(02)2706-6100
網　　址：http://www.wunan.com.tw
電子郵件：shuchuan@shuchuan.com.tw
劃撥帳號：01303853
戶　　名：書泉出版社

總 經 銷　聯寶國際文化事業有限公司
電　　話：(02)2695-4083
地　　址：新北市汐止區 康寧街 169 巷 27 號 8 樓

法律顧問　元貞聯合法律事務所　張澤平律師

版　　刷　2012 年 3 月　初版一刷

定　　價　180 元整